A PIERCING INDIAN CRY SHATTERED THE SILENCE.

The cry was repeated again and again from other parts of the camp as the Indians came alert.

Rifles and pistols thundered inside and outside the tipis; a brave ran from the next tipi toward the horses. Sgt. Casemore led him with his pistol and hit him in the side. The Comanche went down and tried to get up once, then flopped down and didn't move.

Everyone was screaming and shooting. Sgt. Casemore figured it would be a miracle if at least two of the troop were not killed by friendly fire. He rushed from one tipi to the next. Most were deathly silent.

He came out of one and looked back at the Indian he had shot on the run. The brave was not there. The savage must have been faking his wound. He was gone. . . .

PONY SOLDIERS #2

Comanche Massacre

Chet Cunningham

LEISURE BOOKS ∞ NEW YORK CITY

A LEISURE BOOK

Published by

Dorchester Publishing Co., Inc.
6 East 39th Street
New York, NY 10016

Printed in the United States of America

Comanche Massacre

1

Captain Colt Harding kicked the big black army gelding in the flanks and drove him forward through the darkness of the gently flowing West Texas prairie. A night hawk screamed somewhere to the right. His scouts told him they were getting close. Another hour of riding and they would leave their horses and move up.

Colt Harding's moonlit face showed tough and stern. He had been watching this band of Comanches for a week. They had found a small herd of buffalo and stopped for an early hunt. Now the Second Cavalry out of Fort Comfort moved in to rout the hostiles. The Daily Report showed that the date was August 14, 1867.

Captain Harding rode at the front of his forty man "Lightning" company, a fast strike force he had put together that could cover as much ground in a day as any Comanche. His troopers were ready to fight at the end of a sixteen-hour, sixty-five mile ride.

His selected men were tough, hardened, the best shots from all the troopers at Fort Comfort, and they had earned the right to be members of this elite group. They were the best in this section of the famous Second Cavalry. He had hand selected them from the four companies at the fort and created a new unit. Some men didn't want to leave their old company, but the lure of something new and good caught their imagination.

For years the Indians had ridiculed the Pony Soldier for his slow footed mounts, his bugles announcing to the enemy that he was having mess, or going to bed, or getting ready to move, and then the lumbering, slow wagons they always brought along. The Indian traveled light and fast, living off the land.

Now Captain Harding's Lightning force did much the same. No supply wagons trailed his troop. No sabers were allowed, no bugles, no tents for officers or enlisted, and every man carried his own food supply for six, eight or ten days. He took another page from the Indian warfare book.

He brought along five Tonkawa Indians as scouts and hunters. Two of the braves worked ahead, tracking the enemy and picking out the best route for the troop. The other three Indians were free to use their own ponies and only bow and arrow to hunt for food for the company as it rode forward.

On one long trip the Lightning Company had covered seventy-five miles in one day. Few Indian ponies could do better.

Captain Colt Harding was not sure if this was the specific Comanche band he wanted, but any Comanche was fair game. He had been hunting Walking White Eagle and his band for three months now, ever since the chief and a raiding party had caught an army supply wagon train and wiped out all but one on board. The only life spared was that of Sadie Harding, age four, who had been captured and taken away.

Colt Harding wanted his daughter back. The same band had raped and killed his wife, Milly, and cut down his son Yale, who was only six. His family had been on the way from Austin to live on the post with him. Their covered wagon had been attached to the army train with an escort for safety.

Captain Harding had more than a score to settle with the Comanche, and especially the chief called White Eagle!

Captain Harding pulled up sharply as the lead scout materialized out of the darkness ahead. He held one hand high, palm toward the riders.

They stopped and Colt walked his black up to the Indain scout who spoke some English.

"Dismount, walk," the small Tonkawa said. His tribe had "gone to the blanket" on an informal reservation. About ten families lived near the fort and the braves served as guides and scouts for the army.

Captain Harding gave a soft command and the men behind him dismounted. They left three horse guards who tied the mounts together and picketed them by sixes.

The Cavalrymen, more used to fighting from horseback than the ground, grouped around their captain in the dimness. Colt lifted his big pocket watch to catch the moonlight. He checked the location of the Big Dipper and grunted.

"Damn near two A.M.," he said to the men. "We're on schedule. It's about a mile to the Comanche camp. We don't want to take any chances waking them up. We'll spread out when we find the camp and each man pick a tipi and do the job. Remember, check for a five-year-old girl with long yellow hair. If Sadie is in there, I don't want her scratched. We get her out first!''

Captain Harding stared at them a moment in the dim light. "I just pray to God that this is the band that has Sadie. Let's go do it!''

They moved out quietly, hiking the mile in a column of fours much the way they would ride. There was no grumbling in the ranks. They had been trained to move without a sound. No jangling spurs, no coins clinking, no metal clanking on metal. They moved Indian quiet, as Capt. Harding called it.

Every trooper had a Spencer seven-shot rifle. The Spencers didn't have the range some of the longer rifles did, but they could throw out a hail of lead better than any weapon on the market.

A hundred and forty rounds was standard ammunition issue for each trooper to carry. The Lightning members carried two hundred and eighty, and twice the ration, or sixty rounds, for their pistols. About half of them had fourteen inch bayonets on the end of their long gun, and a good fighting knife on their cartridge belt. They were ready.

The lead scout held up his hand and the men stopped behind him. It was still dark, the moon coming in and out behind scattered clouds that scudded to the east.

When they were within five hundred yards of the camp, they came over a small hill and saw the village with a few thin streams of smoke coming from twelve tipis below along a small stream.

The scouts signaled to wait and they moved

forward to check for lookouts or guards. Five minutes later they were back.

"No guards," the lead scout said.

Captain Harding gave the signal for the men to spread out in a line of skirmishers. They were five yards apart as they moved silently down the slope toward the sleeping Indians.

Sgt. Richard Casemore watched his end of the line and motioned three men to move up quicker. There was no talking as the men marched Indian-quiet down the hill.

They had instructions. It was to be a "silent attack" as long as possible. They would use knife and bayonet. Not until the Indians raised a war cry or they fired the first shot were the troopers allowed to use their firearms.

Sgt. Casemore and a private slipped into the tipi at the far end of the camp. A smoldering fire blazed up with the gust of air from the entry flap. A brave lifted up still half asleep. Sgt. Casemore bayonetted him in the chest, yanked the blade out and hit him in the face with a butt stroke of his 47-inch-long Spencer repeater.

A woman darted at him. He slashed her with his knife, then plunged it into her chest through a breast.

Pvt. Vorhees caught up a pair of buffalo robes on a low bed against the wall of the tipi. A ten-year-old boy lay there sleeping. Vorhees slit his throat with his fighting knife and moved to the next pile of buffalo robes. There were no more Indians in the tipi.

Sgt. Casemore motioned outside and they ran to the next tipi only to find two troopers coming out of it, one laughing softly, the other, a recruit who was on his first action with the Lightning troop, looked sickly green even in the dim light. He rushed to one side and threw up.

A piercing Indian war cry shattered the silence of the Texas creek bottom. The cry was repeated again and again from other parts of the camp as the Indians came alert.

Rifles and pistols thundered inside and outside the tipis. A brave ran from the next tipi toward the horses. Sgt. Casemore led him with his pistol and hit him in the side. The Comanche went down and tried to get up once, then flopped down and didn't move.

Everyone was screaming and shooting. Sgt. Casemore figured it would be a miracle if at least two of the troop were not killed by friendly fire. He rushed from one tipi to the next. Most were deathly silent.

He came out of one and looked back at the Indian he had shot on the run. The brave was not there. The savage must have been faking his wound. He was gone.

Sergeant Casemore pointed at three privates.

"You three, over there beyond that brush. Go find their horses and don't let them get away. Go now!"

The three trotted away.

At the other end of the camp, just as the attack began, Captain Harding and a private slipped into the farthest tipi. They let their eyes adjust to the dark interior. The gust of outside air brought two adults upright among their buffalo robes.

Captain Harding grunted with pent-up hatred as he drove his bayonet toward the Comanche brave. The man twisted but the bayonet struck him in the side, daggering under his arm directly into his heart. The brave gave a small cry and fell dead.

The private slashed at a small Indian woman who brandished a knife. He jumped back and then slammed ahead with the butt of his rifle, crushing her skull.

Two children whimpered to one side. Captain Harding ran to them, threw off the robes, but found only a pair of Indian children under five.

"Kill them!" he spat at the private and ran out of the tipi flap. He charged the next tipi just as Corporal Nellington ran inside. A brave had started to come out. His knife caught the corporal in the side.

Before the trooper could react, Captain Harding's knife drove four inches into the brave's neck. A geyser of blood sprayed from the wound, painting all three of them. Slowly the brave sagged, then fell away.

Corporal Nellington staggered. Harding caught him and looked at the blade in his side.

"Easy boy, take it easy. Sit down over here." He eased the trooper to the ground. "Take your kerchief off and fold it into a pad. I'm going to pull that blade out and you put the pad over the wound and press it tight. You do that and you'll be just fine. You hear?"

There was no shooting yet. All was quiet in the camp except for a grunt and a gush of the final breath as another Comanche died.

Corporal Nellington nodded. Harding pulled the knife free. It had penetrated only two inches. The Captain saw the compress held in place, then he ran on inside the tipi.

A woman fitted an arrow in a bow and started to draw the string. Captain Harding charged, batted away the bow and bayonetted her in the chest.

"Your people killed my wife!" he hissed at her.

A second woman came from the side with a knife before he could jerk out the bayonet. He ducked under her charge, slammed his fist into her belly, then jolted the knife from her right hand by grabbing her wrist and elbow and breaking her arm over his thrust up knee.

She cried out and he smashed a backhanded blow against her face, driving her to the side.

The piercing Comanche war cry came then and was repeated again and again. The woman with the broken arm below him screamed the cry. Shots thundered around the camp.

Captain Harding pulled his service pistol and shot the woman once in the chest, then hurried around the tipi. He found three children, one only a baby. He shook his head, holstered his weapon and hurried out.

He saw only a few Indians running. They were quickly cut down by the sharpshooters.

Suddenly there were no more targets. The clouds shifted off the moon and they could all see better.

Sgt. Casemore sent teams into the tipis to check each one. The men were to look for wounded and living and dispatch all quickly, and count the dead.

A half dozen shots slammed through the early morning quietness as the troopers went about their grim task.

Captain Harding ran from tipi to tipi. Nowhere did he find one with the giant eagle's head painted on it, the symbol of Walking White Eagle. He found the largest tipi—it would be the chief's—the leader's.

Inside he saw only the dead. One brave and three women, and four children. All the small ones were Indian. He shuddered, then left the place.

Sgt. Casemore waited for him outside.

"We've checked every tipi, Captain. Sadie just isn't here. My men report that one brave got away. The rest of the Comanche will know you mean business now. They'll know we can fight the same way they can and show no mercy."

Captain Harding nodded. The rush of emotion was gone. The killing lust had been washed away with blood. His vengeance was dulled.

So much killing!

But the Comanche had asked for it!

So many dead!

Not a fraction of the number the Comanche kill!

The children!

Comanche love to swing white babies by the heels, bashing their brains out!

He turned away. "Very good, Sergeant Casemore. Destroy everything here. Start by burning down each of the tipis. It works best to start the fire inside along the walls."

Captain Harding walked back up the hill thirty yards away from the nearest tipi and sat down.

Why did he feel so old? He was thirty-two and felt right now like he was a hundred. Sgt. Casemore would take a body count without being told. He was a veteran.

He watched as the nearest tipi began to smoke out the smoke hole at the top, then one whole wall burst into flames. The carefully-stitched-together tanned buffalo hides made a crackling, hot fire. They burned the tipi poles in half and soon the whole structure fell in on itself.

Any bodies inside would be cremated.

Just as well.

The sons of bitches had asked for it!

He watched another and then another tipi surge into flames until all twelve of them were blazing. Captain Harding called his orderly, Corporal Swenson. They had become separated in the fighting. Swenson had to pass the riding and shooting tests the same as the other troopers to win his place in the unit.

"Lance, see that Marlin takes care of our wounded. Then bring me a count of the casualties. I didn't see any of our men killed, did you?"

"No, sir, but several were wounded." He saluted smartly to a half hearted wave, and left at once.

Colt Harding stared at the burning tipis. Leave them nothing to live in—no tipis, no robes, no food, no horses. Destroy them utterly! They had asked for it! The fires below burned together, some tipis falling sideways onto others.

In the firelight he could see the drying racks where fresh buffalo meat had been cut into strips and hung in the sun to dry. They must have had a good hunt yesterday. Everyone hunts and butchers in a tribe. Everyone was tired this night.

Everyone died, all but one.

He shook his head to clear it. That was his job, killing the hostiles. He would report the attack, detail his methods and wait for any criticism from the brass. He did not follow procedures, but he wiped out an entire band of Comanche—did not just kill two bucks and chase the rest for a hundred miles and never see them again.

He had not followed procedures. He knew he was supposed to do it the way the army had been doing things for a hundred years.

Maybe that's why the Indian was making fools of the army.

No, he couldn't say that. He had found a way to beat the Indians without massive sweeps and thousands of troopers, cannons, wagons, and long supply lines.

He put his chin on his hands that rested on his knees. Perhaps if he closed his eyes for just a few minutes.

"Sir!"

Captain Harding stirred, his chin came off his hands and he looked at his orderly. He saw him silhouetted against an almost daylight sky.

"Sir, Sergeant Casemore has a report."

The First Sergeant of the Lightning troop came up the last ten yards and saluted his commander.

"Sir, we have five wounded. One trooper is dead, Private Ben Zedicher. He was surprised by three braves when he entered a tipi just after the first war cry."

"Enemy dead?"

"We counted forty-nine bodies, sir, before the fires began. That was thirty-one . . . ."

"I don't want a breakdown, Sergeant. Make the report read that forty-nine Comanche were killed in the attack, twelve tipis destroyed and the rest of the village. How many horses?"

"We've captured a hundred and twelve horses, sir, and fifteen mules. Included in that figure are seven branded U.S. army remounts."

"Noted, Sergeant." Captain Harding looked down at the smoking ruins of the camp. "I want everything destroyed. Don't leave one stick another Indian can use. The drying racks should be burned, the meat thrown in the river.

"Save a bale of the jerky. We'll test it on the

way home. The rest of it burn or dump in the stream. Crush every cooking pot, kettle and clay dish you find. Nothing is to be left!"

"Yes, sir."

Captain Harding looked up.

"Sir, I've taken the liberty of sending for our mounts. The men could use a day of rest if it's all right with the captain?"

"Yes, right. When we're done here, pick out a camp upstream half a mile and we'll catch up on our sleep. Tomorrow morning we'll head back to the fort."

Cpl. Marlin came by a short time later with a medical report. Only one man was in serious condition, but he could ride.

"We had one dead, sir."

"Yes, we'll have to bury him here. I'll read a service at sundown. Have two men dig a grave. I want it six feet deep."

"Yes, sir."

Captain Colt Harding watched the final destruction of the camp as it grew light. Nothing remained. Tipi poles not burned completely were set on fire to help burn the bales of jerky and more robes that were found.

Bastards gonna find out we can fight as dirty as they do!

He looked the other way, down the small stream, along the little valley to the rolling hills. Texas.

Goddamn Texas! It had stolen away his family! It had killed Milly and Yale. It had kidnapped little Sadie!

He looked north and west. Up there somewhere must be his little baby girl. Somewhere, and with the savages. He prayed that she had not been harmed. Comanches did terrible things to slaves sometimes.

I'm coming, baby! I'm going to rescue you!

He looked down at his hands. His hands and arms, even his face was still red with the savages' blood. He went to the stream to wash away the blood and came back for a clean shirt. It was one of the few luxuries he allowed himself on his ride. It would soon be time for the men to eat their breakfast.

He wondered if any of them would be hungry. For just a moment he thought of how furious he had been when he killed that last Indian woman. Then he turned away. He couldn't think about that. They had brought it on themselves.

2

Captain Colt Harding did let the men rest upstream from the site of the ruined Indian camp. As usual after a deadly battle, the five Tonkawa scouts were nowhere to be seen. Captain Harding did not even think about what they were doing.

The other Indians on the plains called the Tonkawas the People Eaters. They were. Right now they were up in the hills somewhere having a feast, steaks or a stew or at least soup made from parts of one of their mortal enemies, the Comanche.

They would be back in a day or two, happy, eyes sparkling, making small jokes among themselves. They would ride in and assume their duties as if they hadn't been away. A curious mixture of savage and civilized man.

At first Captain Harding had forbidden the Tonks from any "soup." But soon he realized it was an impossible order to enforce. Now he tried to ignore them.

The morning after the attack on the Comanche camp, the Lightning troop began the homeward journey. There was no great rush going this direction and they moved about thirty miles a day.

Three days later, Captain Harding had the report he was going to write on the attack well in mind. All he had to do was put it down on paper. The tough part would be what the people over at the headquarters of the Department of Texas in San Antonio had to say about it.

Colt Harding was not a huge man. He stood just a little over six feet tall and weighed one hundred and eighty-five pounds. He was lean and fit, with short cropped brown hair, brown eyes under heavy brows. Lately he had gone to wearing a thick, full moustache. He liked it.

Colt had been in the military all his life. Just out of high school in New York, he had won an appointment to West Point. He graduated in 1860, just in time to get a year of experience before the onslaught of the Civil War. He had been a company commander and quickly rose to bird colonel rank before the war was over, getting in on some of the bloodiest battles in that epic struggle.

Because of his West Point background he was reduced in rank only to captain at the end of the war. He saw many of his friends cut down to lieutenant and even master sergeant as the war machine with over two million men was reduced to about twenty-five thousand. His record was part of the reason he held his rank. The army wanted him to stay in. They would need good officers with experience.

Now after eight years in the army he was still a captain, but he knew he was on the new promotion list. He could only wait for the middle of December and pray.

Captain Harding led the troopers into Fort Comfort after the three day march. Their guideon with the special lightning bolt and the Second Cavalry emblem flew smartly. The men were not tired and made a grand entrance. The rest of the troopers were there to greet them.

Fort Comfort was still being built, but it was already a substantial anchor for the defense of Western Texas. The fort stood near the White River a hundred and twenty miles west of Austin.

It was officially a "wilderness" fort, since there were no settlers or ranchers within sixty or seventy miles of the place. It was not near any trails west, but the army decided there should be a defensive fort there to help ward off the active Comanche war and raiding parties, so the fort went up.

Usually there were about two hundred men stationed at the fort. They had four companies, including the newly formed Lightning troop, and not all were full. As usual they were short on officers, and greatly short on officers with experience fighting Indians.

Fort Comfort was built in the form of a square. Three of the sides were finished, made of tough, practical native Texas clay and straw that the Texans called adobe. It was formed in boxes and set out to harden in the hot Texas sun. When baked dry the large brown slabs were almost as tough as red bricks.

The adobe bricks were eighteen inches long and four thick. They were laid up with adobe mortar into a wall two feet thick that would stop any rifle bullet, and probably a five inch cannonball.

Inside walls of Fort Comfort were a foot thick

23

with timbers spanning a 24-foot wide reach to the outer wall. This formed large rooms around the whole square.

Each side of the fort was about 300 feet long. Roofs consisted of tar paper over roofing lumber, and then a foot thick layer of soil on top of the paper and that covered with native wood.

The outside fort wall was three feet higher than the roof to afford troopers a parapet to fire over if they needed to.

One of the corners of the quad was not finished yet. It would eventually be home for the tack room, the fort smithy, inside stables, and the future sutler's store. The south side of the wall had the stable entrance that let the horses into the paddock that extended the full 300 feet along the fort's south wall.

Four strands of barbed wire and sturdy posts kept the stock controlled in the paddock.

Now Captain Harding rode through the main gate, took the sentry's salute and turned the troop over to Sgt. Casemore. He rode directly across the parade ground and past the tall flag pole in the center to the west side of the compound which was "officer country."

Harding stepped down from his black, gave the reins to Cpl. Swenson and walked into his Fort Comfort Officer's quarters.

The whole west side of the fort was assigned to officers, their quarters and their families. Married and single officers lived here. There had been only three married officers on the post when he left.

The north side of the fort was enlisted men's quarters with the barracks, a day room and the mess in the far corner. Around the corner on the east side of the fort stood the kitchen, the ordinance shops, guardhouse and quartermaster and his supplies. On the roof over the quartermaster stood the guard lookout tower.

Beyond the gate was the partly finished area of the sutler's store. When the rest of the southeast corner of the fort was finished it would hold the new sutler's store and the inside stables and additional quarters for married enlisted men and guests.

Captain Harding dropped his cartridge belt on the desk in his office room, and continued on into his private quarters. For a moment he expected to hear Milly's sweet voice and the strident young voices of his children . . . .

He slumped in his chair, his hands over his face for a moment.

"Damnit, damnit, damnit!" he said, each word with more force and more anger. Then he gave a long sigh. One day at a time. That was all he could count on now. Slowly he settled down. He would go out to the office, check for dispatches and new orders, then have a long hot bath and a big dinner and a long night's sleep.

Two packets had come from Austin while he had been gone. Lt. Riddle, his adjutant, had laid them out neatly on his desk. On top of them was a single sheet of paper.

"Finally got that new captain for A Company. Arrived three days after you left. His name is Morse Kenny. He came from artillery, and just did two years in San Antonio at our department headquarters. Guess I'm going to have to go to San Antonio to get my promotion."

That was another job Colt knew he had to do, get John his captain bars. He was long overdue. A fort this size needed a captain to be adjutant.

Of course it also needed at least a major to be commander.

He sorted through the dispatches. Mostly routine. Nothing that couldn't wait. Cpl. Swenson came in. He had washed up and changed his shirt, ready for work. He was a good man. As soon as there was approval for another sergeant on the post, Swenson got the stripe.

"Lance, look these things over and sort them out for me, would you? I'm heading for a long bath."

"Yes sir. Oh, I have a message for you from Doc, er Captain Jenkins." He handed Colt a folded piece of paper. "I'll get some bath water hot for you, sir."

Colt Harding opened the hand written note.

"Colt: Lt. Young and I invite you to supper at the Youngs tonight at six. The new captain, his wife and daughter will be on hand for introductions. Hear you provided me with some work on five troopers. See you tonight."

Colt nodded. Just as well meet them now and then get back to work. He had to whip the whole fort into shape for a visit by Colonel Sparkman, their Texas Department Commander. He was coming in October and already it was September 14, 1868. Damn, the time slid past so quickly!

He had a few minutes until the wood fire heated the copper boiler on top of the kitchen stove. Someday he wanted one of those stoves that had the water pipes running through the firebox! That heated water faster than you would think possible.

Two hours later, he stepped up to the Youngs' door and knocked.

Second Lt. Ned Young opened the barrier.

"Captain Harding, glad you could come. Right this way. We were about to have a taste of sherry before dinner."

Harding stepped into the all too familiar officer's quarters. Each of the ten provided was identical except for his own.

A tall thin man across the room stood stiffly at attention. He had a short haircut, the briefest of a thin moustache, and steely gray eyes. Colt liked the man at once.

"Captain Harding, permit me to introduce you to Captain Morse Kenny," Lt. Young said. "Captain Kenny, our Fort Commander, Captain Harding."

Kenny unfroze, smiled and stepped forward and took the hand that Colt offered. The handshake was firm, honest. Colt liked that about him, too.

"Captain Kenny, good to have you with us, finally. I understand you know something about artillery."

"Afraid so. That won't help much here. But I've had a good basic background in cavalry. Commanding a cavalry company is at least my second favorite job in the army. As you know if a man can get even his third choice he's lucky."

The men all laughed. To the side stood the women. Now Captain Kenny motioned that way.

"Captain, may I introduce you to the best army wife this side of Chicago, my wife, Ruth. Ruth, this is Captain Harding."

Colt saw a plain woman, on the small and short side, with a shy smile that helped brighten her face. She nodded and curtsied but did not offer her hand.

"Mrs. Kenny, good to meet you. We've been

27

waiting three months for the army to decide to send us someone and we are delighted. About time this post had some pretty ladies about.''

She nodded again but said nothing.

"The young lady next to Ruth is our daughter, just turned eighteen, Pamela. She'll be with us only a few months before she goes to her aunt's home in Boston where she'll be attending college, of all things. Pamela, this is our commander, Captain Harding.''

Pamela was slender with a tight fitting dress that showed her off well. She stared straight at Colt and he found her gaze slightly disturbing, challenging. Then she smiled and her face softened into beauty.

"Captain Harding, we've heard so much about you. Is it true you're developing a whole new tactic for Indian fighting? This Lightning unit of yours sounds fascinating.''

She stepped forward and held out her hand.

"It's good to meet you, Miss Kenny. However, I'm afraid that I never talk tactics at a social occasion.''

He took her hand and shook it **gently** then let go. But even as he did there was **a** spark of electricity that jolted through him. This was a most unusual girl.

"That's my Pamela,'' Captain Kenny said, steering Colt toward the sherry. "I guess all my army talk over the past eighteen years has had an effect on her.''

Soon they had dinner, prepared by Mrs. Young. She was a fine cook, and what she did with the issue rations was remarkable. She had used some of her precious canned goods, Captain Harding was sure. He would see that her supply was replaced from the mess.

It was an enjoyable meal. The men talked over cigars after supper, and Colt further discovered things about Morse Kenny that he liked. He was sure that A Company was in good hands. Now all he had to do was get four more officers and he would be nearly up to strength.

Each of his three companies had only one officer each. The regulations called for "one or two" and he always liked two. He had no officer for his Lightning troop, which he commanded himself. He might keep it that way, at least until he got some response from San Antonio about his highly unusual methods of Indian fighting.

Colt begged off early after dinner, and Doc walked him back toward his quarters.

"I like this Kenny," Captain Dr. Jim Jenkins said. He was forty-one years old, had a grown family and his wife was with a sister in the east. Doc liked it that way.

Colt nodded. "Seems to be a good man. I like the way he sits his saddle. We'll get along well together." He paused. "That girl of his is going to be another matter. I'd guess she's a bit on the wild side."

"You noticed. She isn't subtle at all, is she?" Doc rubbed his jaw. "Yes, Colt. I'd say within two weeks we'll be having some kind of problem with Miss Pamela." He hurried on. "Not with me. I'm a married man. Young and Edwards are, too. Lieutenant Riddle is as well. Doesn't leave her much of a field."

"A girl like Pamela will find a way," Colt said, realizing it was true.

Pamela Kenny had been bored at the dinner. Not a man in sight she could talk to, or flirt with.

She smiled as she slipped out of her knee length drawers and stood in her bedroom for a moment absolutely naked. It was a glorious feeling.

Gently she let her hands rub up from her flat little belly to her large breasts. Oh yes! It wouldn't be long before she would have someone help her do that. Just rub and pet her breasts until she almost exploded!

She slipped into her nightgown. A week. She would give herself a week to pick out a target. Once she had selected the man, she would begin to court him, without him or her parents or anyone on the post knowing!

She giggled when she thought about all the fiddle faddle her mother and father spouted about the difference between the enlisted men and the officers.

After spending all her life on army posts, she still couldn't find a bit of difference. Well there was one. There always were a lot more enlisted, and almost none of them were married! This was going to be an interesting assignment for her father—and for her!

The next morning, Pamela dressed carefully. She chose her brown calico with buttons up the front. It was so tight it almost hurt, but it showed off her breasts delightfully. She pinched in the waist and pinned it in back so the small safety pins wouldn't show. It gave her a curvy figure she knew would bring stares. Pamela just loved to be looked at.

By ten o'clock she had found her way around to her father's A Company office. It was a small room where the company records were kept, and a corporal sat helping with the army paperwork. Her father and Cpl. Vic Gregory were going over the rosters and assignments.

"Daddy, you could at least introduce me," Pamela said after she walked in and Victor stood up, but her father only waved and went back to work.

"Oh, sorry. Corporal Gregory, this is my daughter Pamela, Corporal Victor Gregory, our company clerk.

He stood and nodded, but when she held out her hand, he took it and held it a bit too long.

"Yes, now, Corporal, we have a lot of work to do. Pamela, nice of you to visit. You should be helping your mother with the unpacking."

"She wanted me to tell you dinner will be promptly at 12:15."

He ushered her out, but not before Pamela had managed to wink at the corporal when her father couldn't see her. All the way back to her quarters, Pamela memorized Cpl. Gregory's features, the shy little way he grinned, his soft blue eyes and brown hair. He was tall, not as tall as her father, but plenty tall. He was a little on the slight side.

For one quick hot moment she wondered how he would look naked. She put her hand over her face for a second, giggled and hurried on to her quarters, where she flew into the unpacking.

Dr. Jim Jenkins checked the last of his five patients. He had no real infirmary, only two unused visitors' quarters he had commandeered. Two of the wounded would be released as fit for duty tomorrow, but the other two were more serious.

Cpl. Nellington had taken a deep stab wound. He was lucky the savage's blade missed all vital parts, only grazed his small intestine and slid a millimeter past his lung. He would need two weeks of rest.

Jenkins put his feet up on an ammo box and stared at the wall. His wife, Etta, would be going to some tea this afternoon. Then perhaps a bridge or whist game tonight. He had spent enough time at both to last him forever. When he got this Texas assignment out of San Antonio, he had urged Etta to go back to Philadelphia and stay with her sister.

He was glad he did. Yes, he missed her, but his sexual needs were muted now. A once a month romp with one of the laundry women kept him in line, and helped out her finances.

He had tried to talk to Etta about this side of him, but it was simply not the sort of thing he could do, nor would Etta have understood. To her, sex was something done in the dark, in their bedroom, only at night, preferably with her eyes closed and flat on her back with a grimace on her face. A duty not a pleasure.

Poor Etta.

He grinned, but not so poor him. He sobered, thinking about Pamela. She was a pretty girl, ripe for picking, and from what he saw tonight eager to get on with learning about sex. She was going to be trouble, he knew it.

At least it wouldn't affect him. He walked over to his wards and checked the men in the beds. Three of them were sleeping. Nellington still had a lot of pain. Doc dug out a pair of sugar pills and had Nellington take them with a glass of water. The water would do more than the pills to settle him down. Amazing sometimes how a placebo would help.

He watched the ward for ten minutes and when he left, Nellington had dropped off to sleep.

Back at his quarters, Colt Harding lit the lamp on his big desk and looked over the roster. One more officer, that would help. He needed at least two more good officers. And he wanted John Riddle to get his captain's bars. He was due.

He would put another promotion request through tomorrow. He stood in front of a big map of Western Texas and put a red topped pin at the approximate location where they had wiped out the small band of Comanches.

Others pins showed on the map. One was the Wagon Wheel Massacre where his wife and son had died. He had thirteen blue pins there for the troopers who had also died. Large, yellow headed thumbtacks showed frequent sightings of Comanche bands. There were a dozen yellow tacks indicating hunting grounds, hunting camps, summer camps and two for winter camps where the Comanche felt the most safe.

He searched the area, wondering where White Eagle and his band were camped. He'd give six months' pay to know for sure where they were. At least he was learning a lot about Indians on this campaign. He had talked at length to Hatchet, one of the lead scouts from the Tonkawa who could speak some English.

Most of the plains Indians did little during the winter except try to stay warm and have enough to eat. They found safe winter camps with plenty of wood and water in a faraway spot and nearly hibernated for the winter. There was no fighting, no raids, no attacks during winter.

In the spring they left their winter camps to find fresh grazing for their herds of horses and to find new hunting areas. They nourished themselves and their horses into the best of health, and by

May or June were ready to make war on an enemy tribe, to raid another tribe to capture women and children, or to raid the white eyes for women and horses.

Early summer was the time for raiding and war. This period was the glory time for the braves and lasted all summer. Most of the Comanche bands moved often, sometimes twice a week, searching for grazing and new hunting grounds.

When fall came the plains Indians suddenly called a stop to inter-tribal warfare. Their warriors did not kill white eye settlers or ride for women and horses.

Almost by agreement the Indians said, enough war, it is time to go hunting and lay in our winter's food supply. Sometimes, mortal enemies in the spring and summer would battle the mighty buffalo side by side without a harsh word spoken.

Hunting continued as long as the winter food supply was not adequate, or until the shaggy buffalo wandered too far out of the reach of the tribe.

Then the tribe went to a new winter camp, snuggled down in their tipis, found wood for their fires and hoped that the food lasted until spring.

Winter! The ideal time to attack the Indian! Catch him when all of the warriors were at their ease on winter camp. Hit them in all their winter camps and wipe out the whole Comanche nation!

Eventually he would find the White Eagle band, and Sadie, and he would have his little girl home again!

3

Walking White Eagle stood looking across the land that had been Comanche hunting grounds for as long as the old men and their fathers' fathers could remember. He had brought his Eagle band high in the Texas plains, even above the Red River, where the white eye and the Pony Soldiers never came.

He needed peace and a resting time. Time for his band to get back to the old ways and to live as their fathers did, fearing no one, ready to ride and battle with any other Indian tribe.

White Eagle wanted a few months without worry of the white eye captain and his Pony Soldiers in blue shirts.

Even after the surprise attack by the Pony Soldiers, his band was strong and had grown again until now he had more than forty tipis scattered along the tributary of the Red River. He had found a small, virgin valley, where he figured that no Comanche band had made camp in for two men's lives.

The grass was lush and nourishing for the

ponies. The stream bright, chattering and pure. The sky was so blue he knew it was coming to the crisp fall days. There were still many berries, some crab apples and even a few wild walnut trees someone had planted long ago. And there was more game than they had seen in months.

His band had been grievously wounded by the attack by the Pony Soldiers and the captain who wore two pearl handled shoot-many-times-short-guns. They had lost twelve warriors, and several women and children in the attack by Pony Soldiers two months ago.

It had been a terrible defeat. Only the softness of the victors had prevented the losses from being shattering. If the Pony Soldiers had killed the women and children they captured and then had destroyed the tipis, robes and all the food supplies, it would have been a true disaster.

But the Pony Soldiers had not learned to fight the way a Comanche fights. The women and children were spared as was the camp. Now they were rebuilding their strength.

The winter hunt would be coming soon, the last hunt before the demons of winter whistled down out of the hills and tried to bury their tipis in Mother Earth's blanket of new snow.

Another week and they would start their hunt. The buffalo were plentiful in this region, more so than farther south. It would be a good hunt and he prayed to the gods for a short and a mild winter.

Sadie Harding, who now thought of herself more as Laughing Golden Hair, her Comanche name, sat in the soft grass outside the big tipi with the head of an eagle painted on the side.

The sun was warm on her bare back here in

White Eagle's camp. She had two sisters to play with now that she and her mother, Cries In The Morning, had moved into the big lodge with the chief and his family. It was the way of The People. Everyone helped take care of everyone else.

Their old tipi had been given to a warrior and his family who had theirs destroyed by the Pony Soldiers in the surprise raid. For a moment Sadie felt a twinge of doubt. Should she have run to meet the Pony Soldiers when they came? Were they trying to find her to take her back to her beautiful mother and her father who was also a Pony Soldier?

She was confused. Cries In The Morning had been good and kind to her these last three months. She realized that she had never been spanked or scolded since she came to the Comanche camp. The Indian children seemed to do almost anything they wanted to. There was no problem with them.

The Indian children she knew enjoyed their days, played, learned to do what they needed to do to help support the band, but had fun all the time.

How long had she been here now? She thought it had been about three months. She had been through at least three full moons. She remembered that because Cries In The Morning was fascinated with the full moon. She sat outside one night watching it from moonrise until it set early the next morning.

In three months she had learned many Comanche words. She had to just to survive. Now she felt hot and sticky, and ran to the stream and sat with her feet in the cool water.

The September days were still warm, but there was a touch of winter in the air nights and mornings. Soon the snow would come and Laughing Golden Hair wondered what she would do then. How would she stay warm? How did you stay warm in only a tent?

Every time they moved, she had been surprised how much work her mother and the other women did. They did *all the work*! White Eagle explained to her one day that the warriors must be ready at all times to defend and protect the village.

Tradition had built up that the warriors stood at the outer circle of the tipis, with their bows and lances, and now their guns, as the move began.

The women packed up everything in rawhide boxes, and bundles, took down the tipi and formed the travois and packed everything on board. It was simply the way of The People.

Young boys were in charge of the horses. They brought the riding mounts to the women and girls, then drove the spare horses and mules up to the line of march. They were the drovers for the trip, when they weren't playing at being warriors, raiding the village as the women finished their packing, or making a nuisance of themselves.

But the women did not complain when a pretend raid by six teenage boys knocked down meat drying racks, scattered children or disrupted the camp's routine. The young boys were developing the skills and talents they needed before they could become warriors. In a few years the same boisterous boys would be defending the whole camp!

Sadie fingered her braided hair. Soon she would wash it again, let it fly into a blonde halo around her head. She loved her hair loose and blowing in the wind. But Cries In The Morning silently shook her head, chattered about how hair was made to be combed, oiled and braided. Besides, it was less bother braided and did not get in the way of the many duties of a woman.

A half dozen other small girls ran up and urged Laughing Golden Hair to come with them. They were going down by the bend in the stream where the spring runoffs had gouged out a deeper pool where they could sit neck deep in the cool water.

She went with them, thought nothing of dropping her breechclout and jumping naked into the water. Everyone did it. She splashed and dunked the girls and enjoyed herself. Then they ran shivering to the grass and lay in the bright sun letting the rays dry and warm them.

"*Hi, tai,*" one of the girls called. "Hello, friends, there are berries just over there. Let's go eat some!"

They all slipped on their breechclouts and scampered to the bushes that had a berry much like the blackberries Golden Hair had seen before. They were good.

They tired of eating the berries and drifted off. Laughing Golden Hair hurried back to the big tipi, wondering what her mother was doing. She found the small Indian woman hanging out strips of venison to dry in the sun. It was cut thin and would dry quickly. Some venison would not be pounded into pemmican for the winter, but kept in a rawhide box by itself as a treat.

The juicy meat was cut into strips eight to ten inches long, then sliced thin. The strip hung was two inches wide, ten inches long and not more than an eighth of an inch thick. This winter it would be delicious to chew on, that's what Cries

In The Morning told her.

There should be stores, Sadie thought. When her mother had run out of food, she went to the store and brought some home. She looked around. Sadie knew there were no stores here, but there should be. She would ask White Eagle where the stores were.

Before she could, her mother came and motioned for her to follow her.

"Keemah," come, Cries In The Morning said, and they went outside to where the small skin of a deer lay. Together they staked it out, stretching it on the ground, then they did the final scraping on it with a sharp blade of steel that was as big as both of Sadie's hands.

Cries In The Morning carefully showed Sadie how to scrape, so she would not go through the skin, but still remove the last traces of the fat and some flesh that remained.

Then the skin would stand for a day before the tanning process began. Sadie wasn't sure what they used to tan the hides, but the mixture smelled terrible. One of the girls said that they used buffalo brains in a paste that was smeared on. Yuck!

Later Sadie brought water from the clear stream and watched her Indian mother pour some of it into a large copper pot hanging over the fire in the middle of the tipi. Already there were slabs of venison in the pot, and several leaves to flavor it.

Now Cries In The Morning asked Sadie to wash off some wild onions and take off the dried tops. When she had done so, her mother cut them in half and dropped them in the stew.

Sadie hoped there would be carrots and

potatoes as well, but she knew there would not be. The Comanche did not believe in digging in Mother Earth to plant things.

Laughing Golden Hair sat outside in the grass wondering what to do next. She had made friends with her sisters. One was called Black Bird. She was a year older than Sadie, smaller and quick, and with dancing black eyes and loved to play tricks on anyone. But she was a good friend, and they enjoyed teaching each other words.

Her other sister was Something Pretty. She was about Sadie's age and usually they were together. It had been only three months since the Pony Soldiers' raid, but already they were best friends. The other two girls were off doing something for their mothers, and Sadie was alone for a while.

She wondered if her family would ever come and find her. For a moment she relived the terrible day when the bad Indians had attacked the supply train that she, her mother and brother had been with as it drove from Austin out to Fort Comfort.

The noise had been loud, with guns and war whoops. Then an Indian had cut a hole through their wagon and her mother shot him with a pistol. But a minute later another Indian stormed into the wagon and threw her mother out, then he hurt Yale.

The tall Indian had picked up Sadie and carried her under one arm as he went through their goods in the wagon looking for something to steal. He found ribbons and cloth and jumped down from the wagon, satisfied.

Later he had tied her hands and feet together, strapping her across his back like a blanket roll.

That way he could use both hands to loot the train.

By the time the raiding Indians left, Sadie had not seen any of the soldiers alive. Her mother lay on the ground without moving. When was her father going to come and rescue her?

Just as tears began to come, a tall Indian man sat down beside her. White Eagle. He was a most important person in the group and the leader of the Eagle Band. He wore only a breechclout and moccasins. His hair was shiny black, much longer than her father's ever had been.

His face was long and narrow and frowning just a little now.

"Laughing Golden Hair, are you unhappy with The People?"

"I would like to go home," she said softly.

"Your new mother is kind to you, you live in my lodge. You have all to eat you want. What more could you ask?"

She didn't understand all of the words, but she got the idea. She had learned Comanche words as quickly as she could.

"I have a favor to ask you," White Eagle said when she did not reply to his question. "Will you teach me to speak the *tosi-tivo* words?"

"White man's words? Why?"

"Soon the day will come when there will be many white eyes here in Comanche hunting grounds. The white eye and the Comanche will have to learn to live in peace near one another. I have heard how it was with other bands of The People far to the east toward the great waters."

"If I teach you *tosi-tivo* words, will you take me to Austin and let me go free?"

White Eagle laughed. "Your mother would

never let you go. How could Cries In The Morning be happy if she lost you? She has lost her husband. If you left, too, she would sit in the dust and build her last fire and when the small fire went out, she would die with the flames."

"No, no!" Laughing Golden Hair said quickly.

"First the *tosi-tivo* words." He brought out an army pistol from his side. "*Hakai tosi-tivo?*"

"Revolver," Laughing Golden Hair said. She knew about guns. Her father always had guns in the house. Even her mother had one in the covered wagon.

He asked her other questions about the revolver. Soon he knew it had six shots, that the bullets were called shells.

"Pistol shoot six shells," he said in English and beamed. He moved on quickly asking the English words for horse, mule, Cavalry, soldier. They talked about numbers, and she taught him to count in English from one to ten.

"How many horses does White Eagle have?" she asked in English. He frowned, looked at his hands.

"Ten hands many," he said.

She giggled and told him that would be a hundred. She had been good with numbers and could count before she was three.

"You have a hundred horses? You are rich."

Then Something Pretty came and the girls raced off to play hoop ball and chase a buckskin stuffed ball.

White Eagle watched her go. Someday soon she would grow up and become the wife of a great Comanche chief. He hoped it even could be his son, only he had no son. Perhaps Talks A Lot would bear him a son. She would be due soon.

White Eagle arranged for a new set of warriors to go up to the lookouts as scouts. The importance of lookouts had been raised equal to that of warriors, war and raiding. A camp must be safe or the band could be wiped out.

That afternoon he went to the spot his horses grazed on the rich grass and whistled for Flying Wind. His new war pony ran to him quickly, nuzzled his shoulder and accepted having his ears scratched.

There should be one more raid for horses before the Comancheros came for trading. He looked at the herd. He had in his string swift paints, duns, whites, bays, claybanks, and two black Pony Soldier mounts. He could have a good trading, but he would demand rifles and pistols.

The last fight with the Pony Soldiers showed him that the old ways were good, but they could not stand up against an enemy armed with rifles and pistols. The revolvers, as he called them now. could shoot six times as fast as a brave could pull the trigger. They were a tremendous weapon.

He would bargain for more.

Now he put a loose halter on his war pony. Flying Wind was the son of his former war pony, and would be a fine replacement. But first he had more training to do.

When he rode into battle or on a raid, White Eagle wanted both hands free to attack or shoot an arrow or a rifle under Flying Wind's neck while hanging off the side. To do that he had to be able to direct the war pony only with his knees, legs and toes.

It took hours and hours of training. Two other braves worked with new ponies as well in the meadow that afternoon.

White Eagle rode his pony again and again at a good sized pecan tree next to the stream, waiting until the last moment before stopping him with only knee pressure. Then he directed the young horse to turn left or right by knee pressure on one or the other side.

Flying Wind had remembered his previous lessons well. At last White Eagle was satisfied with the colt's progress and took him to a deep growth of special grass where he munched away for half an hour.

When White Eagle came back to his tipi, there was a scurrying around like he hadn't seen in months. Always Smiling was not there. Talks A Lot did not sit in her usual place near the flap. Cries In The Morning was screeching at the three girls. There was no food cooking on the fire. A tanning project had been stopped in the middle.

Cries In The Morning shushed the girls and walked up to him.

"Talks A Lot is ready. She has gone to the birthing hut. You should be a new father shortly." Then she scurried away.

White Eagle stood a moment looking at the dying fire. Then he grinned. Before the sun went down, he just might have a son!

Cries In The Morning hurried up the new path to a quickly made hut barely six feet wide. It was made of sticks and poles, covered with leafy branches woven in. There was a roof of newly cut pecan branches. It had been built only that afternoon when the pains began. It had a kettle of water, a soft cloth, and a matt of branches covered with buffalo robes.

In the center of the hut was the birthing hole, where the newborn would drop. The hole was lined with the softest buffalo calf robe Always Smiling could find.

Only Always Smiling was inside the hut with Talks A Lot. They laughed and cried softly and talked of babies and how much trouble they were and how treasured they were by The People.

"The white eye women breed like field mice," Always Smiling said. "Why can't we have babies the way they do? I've seen their lodges with eight or ten young children in families. That's with just one wife for each man!"

"I don't care how many more children I have," Talks A Lot said. She had passed her seventeenth birthday last week. "Just so this child is a boy! If I can give White Eagle a son he will be so proud!"

Always Smiling sobered. She nodded. That was a problem she had gone through with two other women. They all had hoped for sons.

The pains came again. Talks A Lot bobbed her head. It was time. She straddled the birth hole, squatting so the newborn could come into the world straight down and into the soft fur like robe.

Always Smiling had driven a two-inch stake into the ground beside the hole. It reached up three feet and gave the new mother a firm place to grab hold for balance and to use to help her bear down.

"Sometimes the first child is slow in coming into our world," Always Smiling said. Talks A Lot wiped sweat from her forehead and moved back and sat down on the robes again.

Twice more she waddled over to the birth hole. Then the fourth time, the pains brought forth a scream and she gripped the pole hard and bore down.

A moment later her first born dropped into the birth hole. Always Smiling gathered up the infant, tended to it carefully. She held it bundled in the small robe so Talks A Lot could not see the sex of her child. She rushed the baby out to the stream where a small pool had been diverted so the water would warm in the sun.

There she bathed the perfect, screaming girl baby, and wrapped her in another robe, one of the softest fox fur, and took her back to her mother.

Cries In The Morning had hurried into the birthing hut and tended to Talks A Lot. She lay on the robes over the branches and watched the door.

"I have born a girl child," Talks A Lot said, when Always Smiling came in the door. "Otherwise there would have been much shouting and cheering. The next time I will have a son for White Eagle."

White Eagle did not rush to the birth lodge. Word spread quickly that it was a girl. A girl was of little consequence to a chief, especially to a chief who wanted a son. White Eagle sat on the grass in front of his tipi, near his shield and lance where they could be grabbed up at a moment's notice.

He was young. He would have six sons before he was too old. That's when he decided. He only had two wives after Prairie Flower had been killed in the Pony Soldier raid. He could support another. He would select a new bride soon, one who had two or more brothers. He must have a son!

4

The drums beat a steady rhythm.

The entire camp of the Eagle Band listened and the old women and young men smiled. The young girls hurried through their chores and began deciding which of their prettiest dresses they would wear. Would the soft doeskin fringed with trade beads be best, or the slightly tighter dress with two hundred elk's teeth sewn on it so they rattled with the slighest movement?

The warriors sharpened their lance points, tested their bows and wished they could make new bowstrings from spine sinew of a freshly killed buffalo. Old bowstrings could snap under stress.

A steady stream of warriors came to White Eagle's tipi. They had decided the night before that it was time to go on one more raid for ponies, white women and children before the fall hunting began. Their band could use new blood.

The ponies and horses would be for trade with the Comancheros. White Eagle would take thirty warriors with him. That left twelve warriors to guard the camp, and ten or fifteen teenagers almost ready to be warriors. It would be enough.

The dance would be good for the band. It had been months since they had something to dance about. Now they would all come together around a large campfire, and the dancers and singers would do the ceremonial steps and words to insure a productive raid and safety for all the warriors.

Just after dark the dancing began. Everyone from the band who could get to the big campfire was there—the lame, the injured even the sick. It was an event in the life of the band not to be missed.

The drums had been beating all afternoon and now the special ceremonial rhythm began and quickly the men and women dressed in their finest, formed a large circle around the leaping fire. The men stomped and danced one way around the fire; the women went the other direction.

At times the drum beat changed and then the lines stopped circling and slowly moved toward each other, barely touching whoever was opposite, then moved away and began circling again.

This slow, hypnotic dance continued for more than an hour, then a brave charged toward the fire on his war pony. He shouted a Comanche war cry, and the dancers melted back into the crowd at the edge of the firelight.

The warrior skidded his war pony to a stop at the very edge of the log where members of the council sat facing the fire. The young warrior was Elk Wound, a twenty-three-year-old man who had fought with White Eagle against the Pony

Soldiers in the last skirmish.

He reared his horse up on its back feet and when they came down he shouted the Comanche war cry again. He jumped up and stood on his pony's back, arms crossed.

"We will ride tomorrow as the wind sweeps across the plains. We will strike with the cunning of a fox, and the bravery of a rattlesnake. We will strike our enemies before they know we are there and return home with wonderful presents for everyone!"

Elk Wound went on for aother two or three minutes, explaining in detail how they would slip up on the unsuspecting ranches and even small villages. When he finished, he drove his fourteen foot long lance with a sharp steel point into a circle drawn in the dirt three feet in front of the council.

The lance stuck, quivered in place, and remained upright.

Elk wound dropped to his war pony's back and without touchng the hackamore, charged out of the firelight, screaming another Comanche war cry as he went.

There was much cheering and shouting and stamping of feet. Then the dance began once more.

They danced until after the Big Dipper had fallen out of the sky to the north, then went to their buffalo robes for one last lovemaking with each of their wives before the dangerous mission to come.

Two days later they found a small settlement well down the Red River. They were still far from any other white eyes. These white eyes were challenging them, building lodges and putting up poles to keep their horses in out here deep in the traditional Comanche territory. It was a slap in the face of every Comanche warrior on the raid.

They waited until darkness, then slipped up within hearing distance of the five wooden lodges. They had been made by stacking logs on the side and notching the ends so they stayed in place. Smoke came from the chimneys even though it was still warm outside.

Four members of the council on the raid talked. They had seen eight men among the cabins, many women and children. The council decided they would rest now and attack at dawn. Two of the younger warriors protested.

"We can attack now, rout them in the dark. Kill the men, take the women and children and all of their horses and six of the small buffalo type cows and head back for our camp."

The council argued with the warrior, but he could not be convinced. That was when White Eagle remembered the control that the Pony Soldier captain had over his men. If he gave the order to cease fire, they stopped. If he said go, they went. If he told one group to attack, or to cross the river, there was no discussion, the Pony Soldiers went as ordered.

It was not so with the Comanche warriors. Each man was a force unto himself. His vision quest had told him to be. But it made group operations harder. Most of the warriors knew that a group attack was best, that it needed some form, some strategy. But all too often one or a pair or a group of warriors would become impatient and attack early, or would ignore the plan of the council.

He watched the warriors and most seemed

content to wait to attack until dawn. Many warriors believed that night attacks were dangerous. If they were killed at night, their spirit would forever have to wander in darkness, never being able to find the light and to pass on into the glorious afterlife with their parents and friends.

Most of the younger warriors laughed at such talk. They said there was little danger of even being wounded by the unskilled farmers and rancher white eyes. Most of them could not even fire their weapon accurately.

An hour before sunrise two warriors left their ponies and slipped up to the closest cabin. The five small houses were built in a rough circle, with not more than fifty yards between them across the circle.

White Eagle had been awake for an hour watching the site. When he saw the two warriors leave, he roused the rest and they worked up as close as they could to the cabins. They were in the side of a small valley, and three of the cabins were in the edge of the woods of live oaks and pecan trees.

A scream stabbed through the night.

All was quiet for a moment, then a pistol fired in the nearest cabin, and White Eagle lifted his voice in the Comanche war cry that signalled his warriors forward. Half a dozen had already charged into the darkness, now all of them surged forward.

A white eye staggered out his front door, pistol in hand. White Eagle shot him with an arrow through his heart and leaped to the man's side in time to grab the pistol before he dropped it.

Comanches darted into all except one of the

houses. In that one the people inside had been quick enough to close the door and bolt it in place. Window shutters slammed into place as well over the two windows and for a moment the attackers were stopped.

Limping Crow ran from one of the cabins with a woman. He stopped in the better light and stared at her. She was young, with dark hair and wore a long white nightgown. With his knife he slit the cloth from neck to hem and threw it aside. The woman tried to cover herself.

Limping Crow slapped her and she shrieked, but let him pull the ruined garmet away. Limping Crow nodded, tied her hands and feet with rawhide and dumped her on top of her ruined nightdress. Then he laid one of his arrows across her. The arrow was specially marked with a dotted red line around the shaft near the feathers. It was the Comanche way of marking his goods.

Limping Crow screeched a war cry and raced back into the house. Just inside he saw the man he thought he had killed. The seriously wounded German settler threw a hatchet with deadly aim. The blade of the heavy instrument sliced through Limping Crow's chin, splitting the bone and continuing downward. The blade chopped through his neck, severing his spinal column and stopping at last buried in his chest.

Limping Crow died in seconds.

A second warrior in the cabin lit a fire inside so he could see. He dragged Limping Crow out of the burning cabin, then rushed back in, slit the German's throat and hurried out with a bolt of cloth for his wife.

White Eagle charged into another cabin, saw a man lift a long gun, but before the man could fire,

White Eagle shot an arrow into his chest. When the white eye's finger pulled the trigger, the weapon was aimed at his wife. Her face and chest dissolved in a frothy mass of blood and pulped flesh as she slammed against the wall and fell across the cold stove.

Light began to tinge the east.

White Eagle checked the white eye man. He was dead. He had been clutching a rawhide sack. White Eagle pried it from the stiffening fingers and looked inside. Past the drawstring he found a tumbled group of the same round golden discs he had seen before. Always Smiling had liked them.

The man protected them with his life. How were they so valuable? Did they possess good magic? Were they favored by the gods for their beauty? He shrugged. It was more *tosi-tivo*, more white man's ways he had to learn. He would take the woman's clay and find out about it.

For a few minutes he searched the cabin. He found the shotgun, which he threw aside. It was too big, he had no bullets to fit it. He had never seen a shotgun before.

Beside the man he found two pistols. He took both, tying them to his surcingle. There was a rifle on the wall that the man had no chance to reach. White Eagle took it down and was about to leave the cabin when he heard a small voice.

On the bed platform against the far wall he saw movement in the dim light. He jumped to the bed and pulled off the blanket. A small boy lay there. He was no more than three years. A boy, a son! He scooped the boy up, carried him outside and put him down where other warriors had set loot.

One of the cabins was already burning. He heard a wild scream and then a warrior pulled a woman into the firelight of the cabin. She had been stripped naked. The warrior looked at her for a moment, seemed fascinated by her large white breasts. Then he threw her to the ground and shouted with delight as he pulled loose his breech-clout and mounted the white eye.

There were none left alive in the four cabins. They looked at the last one. Gun barrels came out firing slots. As it grew lighter the warriors would become the targets.

Quickly they left, taking their treasures with them. White Eagle looked at the white woman near Limping Crow's body. The arrow across her chest was his. He picked her up and ran with her and the small boy into the pecan brush out of sight of the last cabin, then sat them down.

"Stay," he told them in English. The woman looked up, her tears dry on her cheeks. She nodded and held the small boy in her arms.

The last cabin was a problem. The weapons coming out of the firing slots were shooting now. No one could creep up near enough to it to set it on fire.

Several fire arrows were shot at the roof, but it would not catch on fire.

White Eagle solved the problem. He went upwind of the cabin, cut green pecan branches and carried them to a fire just inside the fringe of woods. They were twenty yards from the back of the cabin.

Soon the smoldering green pecan leaves produced a thick white smoke that drifted against the cabin rear wall. When the shooters inside were blinded by the smoke, White Eagle and four others rushed the wall, set fire to the brush they had carried with them, and soon the smaller logs on the wall caught fire. More and more brush and small limbs and then larger chunks of wood were piled against the burning wall.

When the entire back wall was burning well, the Indians moved to the side and the front to wait for the victims inside to come out.

None ever did. They heard several shots, but did not know why. When the rear wall burned through and fell inside, they got the front door open. A farmer and his wife and two children lay dead on the floor, all dead of gunshot wounds.

By that time it was full light. The warriors delighted in searching the remaining cabins for treasures to take back to their lodges.

Some took hoes, one a spade, another two new leather halters that could be reworked into war bridles. When everyone was satisfied with the plunder, the cabins were burned down. There was no barn, but in the corral and a small pasture nearby, they found twenty-five horses and six mules. All were rounded up and two young boys brought along for the purpose were assigned to drive the horses back to the Comanche camp. It was too early for the whole party to head back yet.

White Eagle looked at the woman Limping Crow had claimed before he died. White Eagle had rescued her from the exposed position. By rights she was his. He had no need for a slave. She was of child bearing age. He could use her as a brood mare. Yes, a son from her would still be his son!

He caught a horse for her, told her with signs and his few English words that she must care for the boy. She nodded.

Then she pointed at her body. "Clothes?" she asked. He didn't understand. She caught the small boy's nightgown and shook it. "Clothes."

"Clothes," he said, then understood. He went with her back to the ashes and the scattered belongings. She wept as she looked at what had been her home. Her husband was dead somewhere in the ashes.

Quietly she searched and soon found two pair of men's pants that were not too big. They were overalls. She found a woman's blouse. With an effort she put it on. She knew who owned it and a sob caught in her throat. All dead but two of them! She ran back to the big Indian who now "owned" her and stepped on board the pony. No saddle, not even a saddle blanket.

They were several miles down the river before she realized that she had no shoes.

White Eagle pushed the band hard. They found a small farm and bypassed it. Another ten miles down the Red River they found what they wanted, a cattle ranch. White Eagle had eaten beef, but he was not impressed by it. The beasts were too small, and they were not as available as the buffalo.

Still in an emergency a few beef would be handy. And they did not run off.

They attacked the ranch as soon as they arrived. The woman and boy were left to the rear. The battle was over in two minutes. Only three men and two women lived at the small ranch. All were killed and scalped in the fight.

The warriors swarmed over the barns and corrals. There were fifty horses in the corrals. From the looks of them all had been ridden.

The horses were rounded up and after the house

and barn burned to the ground and the corral torn apart, the raiding party headed for home, with fifty more horses and ten of the cantankerous Texas longhorn beef cattle.

It took them four days of hard riding to get back to their hidden valley. White Eagle had allotted the horses to the warriors, then split them into four groups and they took off in different directions, but all headed generally to the west.

Twice White Eagle sent scouts to check their back trail. No one was following them.

The four groups met a day's ride from the camp and moved on together. A mile outside the summer place, they stopped and each man put on his best bit of loot. Some wore fancy jackets, some top hats, some war paint. They sent one man into camp to let them know the raid was over.

At noon they made their grand entrance into camp. White Eagle came first with his captives. The woman told him her name was Doris. She had braided her hair on each side, and since she had not tried to get away, White Eagle untied her hands so she could hold the small boy.

Each night when they stopped, White Eagle had talked to the boy, told him what a bright future he had, how proud he would be to be a Comanche chief. All he had to do was grow and learn and be better at everything than any of the other boys. It would be easy!

The women, old men and warriors left in camp came out to greet the raiders. The girls wore their prettiest dresses, the women danced as they waited, small boys threw sticks at the girls and chased the dogs.

The parade of warriors and their herd of horses and ten steers went through the half mile long stretch of tipis. Flying from proud lances were a dozen scalps. They would be treated before the dance that night. The parade turned at the far end and came back, with each warrior dropping off at his own tipi. The horses were sent to the pasture where boys tended and protected them.

That night the traditional victory dance was held. Again the drummers announced the festivities. When darkness came the dancers assembled and soon the first warrior rode into the circle. A fresh buffalo hide had been spread on the ground near the council.

As the rider charged into the circle scattering the dancers, he drove his lance deep into the buffalo robe, then recounted to all listeners how he excelled in war and raiding, and especially how he had taken his scalp and stolen many horses.

When he finished, he rode out and the next warrior rode in, drove his lance into the buffalo robe beside the previous one and recounted his bravery over the challenges of the enemy.

When the last warrior had given his talk, White Eagle rose from the council log, and told of the death of Limping Crow. The crowd was silent for a moment, then the dancing continued. The name of Limping Crow would never be spoken again in the camp. It would be bad medicine, and bad for his spirit trying to climb out of the small hill where they had given him his above ground burial on the return trip.

There was a new family in camp. A warrior who had been with Bear Claw's band. Any Comanche could live wherever he wanted to. No one could deny a warrior of a family the right to attach himself to one clan or another. It was his right.

When Running Thunder came into the White Eagle band camp, he was greeted as any warrior. As he sat and talked with White Eagle, he asked if the chief knew of a Pony Soldier captain who rode at the head of his column with a pair of white handled pistols.

White Eagle passed the pipe to the warrior, thought for a moment, then nodded.

"I know him. I have seen him. He is different from the other Pony Soldiers. He attacked our camp two months ago. I think the man is half Comanche, the way he moves."

"He has been talking to everyone he finds who travels through our Comanche lands. He tells all he is giving a large reward for the person who brings back to him his small golden haired daughter called Sadie."

"I have heard the same story."

"It is reported that this Pony Soldier has said he will give a hundred horses or two hundred dollars in woman's clay, the gold coins the white eyes treasure so highly."

"I will remember the story," White Eagle said. They rose and he went into his tipi. Usually White Eagle would arrange to sell a slave or a captive at once if it would be profitable.

But not for Laughing Golden Hair. She was a special one. She was the delight of Cries In The Morning. More important, some day Laughing Golden Hair would grow up to marry a Comanche chief and be a great leader of her adopted people.

He watched the small girl for a moment, then went outside. It was not proper for a warrior to pay so much attention to a girl child.

He found the woman, Doris, who was also

staying in his lodge. He told her it was her job to protect and take care of the small white boy.

"Are those my only duties?" she asked. He saw the rise of her breasts, the flare of her thigh, but he nodded.

"For now; your only duties."

5

Captain Colt Harding moved another pin on his wall map showing where a traveler had seen a group of Comanches moving across the rolling Texas prairie. That could put the band anywhere beyond the Colorado River and to the north. He pushed the pin into the map where the last tributary of the Texas Colorado showed on his map.

The three foot square map had become a patchwork of pins where different travelers had seen Comanches. Some of the sightings he believed in but many were probably fanciful imaginations. But which ones were which?

He had been making reward offers to everyone. He could get up two hundred dollars if he had to, but a hundred horses would be harder. It didn't matter.

Anything, he would do *anything* to get Sadie back from those savages! He'd even leave the army if it came to that. Colt thought of the sweet young face, the darting blue eyes, and the long blonde hair that was a perfect match for her mother's. He blinked rapidly and turned away.

He couldn't dwell on that line of thought for more than about thirty seconds.

A double knock sounded on the door and Cpl. Swenson came in.

"Captain Kenny of A company is here to see you, sir."

"Right, send him in, Swenson."

Captain Harding had recovered his composure and his face was set and formal when the A Company commander came through the door.

"Morning, Captain Kenny. You seem to be settling in rather well here at Fort Comfort."

Across the parade grounds, Pamela Kenny had waited patiently for her father to leave the A Company headquarters room. When he went into the fort commander's office, she hurried down from where she had been talking to Lt. Edward's wife. Pamela watched as Mrs. Edwards turned into her own quarters.

Pamela marched into the Company A office and closed the door gently. Cpt. Victor Gregory bent over his desk.

"You might at least invite a lady to be seated," Pamela said with an annoyed lilt in her voice.

Gregory scrambled to his feet, bracing at attention.

"I'm sorry, Miss Kenny. I—I didn't see you come in."

"So where may I sit down?" Pamela asked.

"Sit down?—oh, yes, here, I'll bring a chair." He did, holding it for her. Instead of sitting down she caught his hand and held it. He looked at the door.

"Miss Kenny. Your father is at the fort commander's office. He just went over there."

"I know, silly. I waited until he left. I came to

talk to you. I've only seen you twice since we first met a week ago."

"That's as it should be, Miss. You're officer people."

"That doesn't make a bit of difference to me. I like you, Victor Gregory. I don't care if you're an important general or a private."

She moved around the chair until she stood directly in front of him. "I said I like you. Do you like me? Just a little?"

He lifted his eyes in exasperation. "Land sakes, yes, Pamela Kenny. I think of almost nothing but you. I've been making mistakes, getting into trouble. You're about the prettiest little thing I've ever seen!"

Pamela glowed with the praise, the compliment. She looked up at him, openly, watching his face. "Then why don't you do something to show me?"

"I just told you."

"You might even be so bold as to ask if you could hold my hand, maybe. . . ."

She stopped as she reached over and put her hand around his and gripped it tightly.

"Your daddy walks in here right now and I'm busted back to private!" he said through clenched teeth.

"Oh, poo. I can talk him out of anything." She leaned closer to him, then stepped forward so her breasts touched his chest. He looked down, his eyes wide as sunflowers. Then she put her arms around him, pushed tightly against him from hips to chest and hugged him.

"I been wanting to do that for more than a week now, Victor Gregory!"

His ears were red, he could feel the blush

creeping down his neck. He was aware that there was a hardness crawling rapidly from his crotch and he had no power at all to stop it.

She still held him.

"Do you like this?" she asked.

"Oh—damn!"

Pamela giggled. She reached up and caught his neck and bent his head down. Pamela Kenny stretched up on tiptoes and pressed her lips to his in a quick kiss.

She finished the kiss, touched his chest and stepped back. "I hope you liked that, too, Victor Gregory. If you did, see what you can do about arranging so we can meet sometime, alone, so maybe we can kiss again."

She smiled, twirled around so her long skirt lifted enough to show a flash of leg all the way to her knee, then she went to the door and looked out quickly to see if anyone was watching. There was no one nearby, so she waved to him, winked and slipped out to the walkway.

Pamela continued on around the square to the sutler's store where she had been instructed by her mother to go for some cinnamon.

She walked along, pleased with herself. Victor had been absolutely *purple* when she kissed him. He evidently was totally inexperienced with women. That was fine. She had felt the sudden swelling at his crotch! At least with him things wouldn't get out of hand.

Pamela wondered if he had hair on his chest. Bill, back in San Antonio had lots of black hair. He had let her play with it while he was . . . She smiled and hurried into the suttler's store. It was so small and had little merchandise except staples. It was nothing like the big stores in

Washington D.C. and in Philadelphia. Maybe someday soon she would be back there.

"You must be the new girl," Hans Altzanger, the sutler, said as she came to the small counter.

"Yes, sir. Pamela Kenny. My mother wants some powdered cinnamon."

"Just have one left, Miss Pamela. Anything else today?" That question brought all sorts of strange, wild, crazy ideas to her head, but she shook her long blonde hair.

"Only the cinnamon, thank you. How much is that?"

She paid him seven cents from a small coin purse and walked quickly back to her quarters. This was the night her mother was "repaying" the welcome dinner they had been given. All the officers on the post were invited, and of course, they all would come. It would not be seemly to refuse, partly because there were so few officers.

Captain Kenny was home early that afternoon to help his wife, Ruth, with the dinner. He was quite a cook in his own right when he had the time.

He came into the main room where the table had been expanded with three extra leaves and stared at his only child for a moment.

"Pamela, you could do a lot worse than stay right here at Fort Comfort and set your cap for the fort commander. He's a vital, young man, with good sense and should be a major soon. Do you like him?"

Pamela shorted and stood, so her father could know what a good figure she really had. "Father, Captain Harding is well over thirty."

"He's thirty-two."

"All right, he's thirty-two, which is nearly

twice as old as I am. He's too old for me. Besides, if you haven't noticed, the man is in deep pain and in mourning for his murdered wife and son and his kidnapped daughter. Give the man some breathing room."

Morse Kenny nodded. "Just wanted to see if you noticed. You probably also know which officers on the post are married, and which have wives back east."

"Oh, Daddy. With only seven officers in the whole fort, it isn't hard to figure out. They're all married except the captain. Of course you are four officers short on the roster."

Captain Kenny chuckled. "Is there anything you haven't missed? I guess it will be good for you to go to college. You seem to have more of a head on your shoulders than some junior second lieutenant could handle."

Pamela smiled. "I think you are quite right about that, Father, and the same applies right up to most majors who I have known. Now I should be helping Mother with the dinner."

There were ten for dinner that evening at seven-thirty. Mrs. Kenny had done the cooking. One of the enlisted men's wives, Mrs. Ida Barlow, did the serving.

Captain Harding was there, as well as Dr. Jenkins, and Captain Kenny and his wife. Lt. Edwards and his wife, Olive, sat together as did Lt. Young and his wife, Grace. Lt. Riddle was slightly late arriving. A dressed up and pretty Pamela rounded out the ten. Even if she did think so herself, Pamela knew she was the prettiest lady there. She was also the youngest.

She had arranged so she could sit next to Captain Dr. Jenkins. He would talk the whole time with Pamela's mother since they both hailed from Boston.

On her left was Lt. Young. She had decided to see how much she could tease him that evening without getting angry looks from her mother.

She drew out the twenty-four year old lieutenant, getting him to talk about himself. In the low buzz of conversation no one paid much attention to what the others around the table were saying.

Pamela had been asking more and more personal questions of Lt. Young. Now and then she saw Grace Young bend around her husband and scowl at her, but Pamela ignored it.

She moved and her leg brushed the officer's leg under the table. His gaze darted to her and she touched her mouth with her hand.

"Sorry," she said and continued talking about how she was looking forward to going to Boston. A short time later her leg brushed his again and this time held the contact. She glanced at him and saw color rising up his neck.

Mrs. Young looked around her husband. Her face was flushed with anger, she could barely speak. At last she got the words out.

"Miss Kenny, would you please leave my husband alone!"

There was a moment of shocked silence around the table. Grace Young's strident voice had cut through the talk and everyone heard the words clearly. Quickly Lt. Young rose, took his wife by the hand and led her to the small entranceway near the front door.

He mumbled his apologies to Mrs. Kenny that his wife had not been feeling well all day, and hurried her outside and down the walk toward their quarters.

Pamela had not let the movement affect what she was doing. She had a delicate bite of the roast beef and looked at Dr. Jenkins.

"Doctor, I understand in Boston you had some interesting methods for helping women deliver their babies without pain. Can you explain the procedure to me?"

Doctor Jenkins chuckled, then shook his head. "I'll be glad to when you're at least eight months pregnant, and when we're not eating this fantastic supper that your mother cooked for us."

"Fine, I'll wait," Pamela said.

Her father shot her one of his sternest looks. She had seen it many times before at a company dinner. It was the last warning before he removed her from the table. "Excused!" would be his word for it.

She settled down. No use wasting a good dinner. She especially enjoyed the mashed potatoes and the beef gravy. It was one of the most satisfying evenings she could remember in a long time. If Lt. Young had not reacted the way he did, she would have put her hand on his leg next. That always brought results at the stuffy dinner table gathering.

Captain Kenny had given her a stern lecture after the guests left about her responsibilities as his daughter.

"Somehow you were teasing Lt. Young. I don't know how and I'm not interested in knowing. But, if it happens again, you will never again have dinner with us when we have guests. Do I make that point particularly clear, Pamela?"

"Yes, Father. Clear." She lowered her gaze, as she knew he would expect her to. She could play the obedient child for a few more weeks.

The next morning, Captain Kenny had to hurry off to train his troops. No one brought up the problem she had created at the dinner the night before. After breakfast, Pamela sat near the window and watched her father march across the parade grounds. He was all army officer and always would be.

That same morning, Captain Harding had called out his Lightning Company to train. Their regimen was slightly different than the other troops. Captain Harding was buying ten dollars worth of ammunition a month to use in training.

Most of the army did little or no target practice. It was considered a waste of time, and too expensive to allow. Captain Harding went against the practice, and listed much of the ammunition expended as being used in "patrols and clashes with hostiles, mostly Comanches."

This morning he had taken the forty men of Lightning Company two miles beyond the fort to the east where there was a slight draw where the land leveled out to meet the White River. There he brought them into a company front in ranks of four, ten long and then rode to the long side of them.

"Left turn, Hooooooooo!" Captain Harding called. The men turned their horses toward him so he faced ten men on horseback, four deep.

He signalled the two Tonkawa scouts he had brought with him. The two were the best riders from the Tonkawa camp. One of the Indians jumped off his horse, left it and ran thirty yards ahead. He stopped and looked behind him.

The second scout, still mounted, pounded toward the man on foot at a flat out gallop.

Without losing speed or stride the Tonkawa on the horse scooped up the Indian on the ground, and a moment later he was mounted behind the first Tonkawa and the two rode away.

The members of the Lightning Company shouted and cheered as the successful pickup was made.

The Indians circled and came back. The Tonkawas traded places, with the man who had been on the ground, now riding the horse. They looked at Captain Harding.

"Men, you've just seen a dandy little maneuver that could save your scalplock one of these days. How many of you can pick up a man who's on foot?"

One man lifted his hand. He was a recruit who had been on the post only a short time.

"At least one. You'll have a chance to prove it. Every man in the company is going to learn how to do this before we go in for chow. Is that understood?"

Some of the men grumbled, others grinned. This *was* a maneuver that could save lives in an attack.

The Indians did the pickup again and again, doing it slowly, so the troopers could get the idea. Then the Tonkawas picked up a trooper, told each man how to do it, when to jump, what part of the horse or saddle or the other man to grab.

The first few tries resulted in the Pony Soldiers falling off the horse. One man hit hard and sprained his wrist.

When the first man made it up, everyone cheered. Three hours later each man had been picked up by one of the Indians. Then the troopers began to do the picking up.

Again they followed the example of the Indians, who showed them slowly how to do the job.

The man who said he could pick up a downed man was Pvt. Oxford. Riding at a good gallop, Oxford picked up one of the Tonkawas. Then he explained to the now eager troopers how to do it.

It took an hour before another trooper successfully hauled a downed rider onto his horse. It was not pretty, but it worked.

Captain Harding moved that man with Pvt. Oxford to one side and worked with the rest.

Lightning Company dragged into the fort that night a half hour after dark. But every man was grinning. They had done it! Every man, even Sgt. Casemore and Capt. Harding had both picked up a man and been picked up.

Captain Harding brought them to a company front and rode up and down the line.

"I'm proud of you men! You're proving me right. With good training and the right tactics, we can beat any Indian tribe they try to send against us. Sergeant Casemore, see to it that special chow is served up for your company. You deserve it. Carry on."

Sgt. Casemore snapped a salute to his captain, bellowed out the orders and moments later the men took their tired mounts to the stables where they spent three quarters of an hour rubbing them down with dry straw, and then feeding them a full ration of oats.

"In the cavalry, your mount comes first," Sgt. Casemore bellowed as they began to growl. "That animal is more important than your rifle or your balls! He can save your damned hide." He grinned and slapped a black army mount on the

73

rump.

"Chow is fifteen minutes, just in case anybody is interested."

Captain Harding ate the cold supper Cpl. Swenson brought him, fell into bed and slept without waking until five A.M. He rolled over and tried to go back to sleep. He ached in every bone. His arms felt like they would drop out of their sockets.

He groaned as his feet hit the rough floor boards. Then he grinned. At least he knew how the rest of the Lightning Company felt. He had fallen twice before he learned how to help to be picked up on a charging army mount.

When he tried to pick up a man he nearly lost his saddle again. It took him four tries to pick up a trooper. Then he did it four times in a row to prove to himself that he really knew how.

Today they would learn how to shoot from a horse, Comanche style. For that he needed a hot breakfast.

He went to the mess hall and to the small officers mess at one end where he ate half a dozen eggs, sunny side up, six thick slabs of bacon, a stack of hot cakes and three cups of coffee.

The troop sat in the sun waiting for him at six-thirty when he came out of his quarters.

"Lightning Company all present and accounted for, sir and ready for training," Sgt. Casemore bellowed.

They rode smartly out the gate and toward the same draw they had used before. This time the Tonkawa Indian scouts demonstrated how to hang off one side of a pony and shoot a rifle under the horse's neck. After years of riding with both boots in both stirrups, it took a lot of practice to ride with one.

At last one of the men hooked his left knee around the saddle horn, then he had the balance to lean down and fire under the horse's neck with one hand on the Spencer.

The men rode by single file, five yards apart on dry runs, trying to get their balance.

Captain Harding called them together. When he organized the Lightning Company, he had broken the company down into four squads of ten men each. A corporal was leader of each squad.

He glared at them. "I hope to hell you men have a little more respect for the Indians when they ride at you off their mounts so all you can see is a foot and an elbow. It's damn tough. Our problem is that the Comanches are way ahead of us. They have been learning how to ride this way since they were five years old.

"They ride without either hand, and can draw a bow and arrow and hit what they aim at, under the damn pony's neck." He walked his big black around in a circle for a moment.

"All right. We're not going to learn how to do this today. For the next three days, I'm leaving each corporal in charge of practice of his squad. Four days from now we'll have a live firing test, to see how many of you can pass it. Every man of every squad will pass, or he's out of the company. The squad that shoots the best score on the target will get a hundred extra rounds for target practice."

"Any questions?"

Sgt. Casemore lifted his hand. Captain Harding nodded.

"Sir, can we have one of the Tonks for each squad as an instructor?"

"Done." Harding looked around. Already the men were talking it up, making side bets. He grinned. Sometimes there was more than the field manual way to get a job done.

He led the company back to the fort just in time for the midday meal of salt pork, potatoes, and beans.

Captain Harding slumped in his chair in his office and stared at the map of West Texas on his wall.

Where was she? Where in hell and in Texas was his little girl, Sadie?

6

The man had to be at least sixty, Captain Harding thought as he looked at him across the desk. His hair hung around his shoulders in dirty strings, his beard scraggly, uneven. A sore on his cheek had not healed and his face was burned dark from the sun and the wind. His eyes squinted almost shut from long experience in self preservation, but he chuckled as he looked up at the cavalry officer.

"Yeah, I know what yer about to say. But don't bother me a twit. Sure, I know I'll probably never find that one big strike, or even a little one. Still, could be some silver in these washes and the low bluffs. Man's got a right to try. Too damn cold out there in the real mountains.

"Had my fill of Californi and Nevader. Nuff of them places. Warmer come a summer in Texas." He took a bite off a plug of dark chewing tobacco and nodded.

"Thankee for the chew, been nigh on to a month since I had some. Finally used some cactus skin offen some of them big wide parts. Tough as all hell it was, but didn't taste none too bad.''

Captain Harding poured another two fingers of his best Kentucky bourbon into a glass and handed it to the prospector. He sipped at it as if it were a great luxury he wanted to last as long as possible.

"Getting back to the Comanche, Mr. Thayer. They don't bother you, you say. You can ride right past their camp, or even stop by for a smoke on their pipe."

"Right as rain, sonny. They know I ain't gonna move them out of their lands. Know I ain't gonna start farming or use up all the game. I'm no threat."

"Can you show me where you've been lately, and where you've seen any Comanche camps?"

"Reckon. You the feller hunting the little white girl captive?"

"That's right. She's my daughter. Her name is Sadie Harding, she's five years old by now and has been gone over three months."

"Mmmm. Reckon she's safe. Comanche like to steal kids to adopt to some squaw with no youngens. Done all the time. Treat them like bone china. Never seen a Comanche hit a kid, or scold one bad even. Kids are damn important to the Comanche. The squaws don't drop many kids of their own, you see—"

"Where have you been prospecting, Mr. Thayer?"

The old man stood with a bit of a hitch, then went to the wall map slowly.

"Well, now I came back down the Colorado here, the Texas Colorado that is, not the big one over in Colorado and Utah and Arizona and Californi. Didn't see but maybe one band in there.

Don't know for sure who it was. Tipis was up when I went by."

"Did the biggest tipi have an eagle head painted on it?"

"Nope, sure didn't. That'd be White Eagle's band. Met him once or twice. Big son of a bitch."

"Where did you go from there, Mr. Thayer?"

"Hit the hills for a while, then down to the White River and here I am."

"Before the Colorado?"

"Yeah, I went up Beaver Creek off the Wichita, then the North Fork of the Wichita all the way to the Caprock that protects the Staked Plains. Saw two or three Comanche bands up in there." He frowned for a minute, his eyes almost closing. "Nope, don't remember no eagle tipi up in there neither."

"Mr. Thayer, I would be grateful if you would keep an eye out for the Eagle Band. I'm sure that's the group that stole Sadie. I'm not sure they still have her, but it's likely." He stood and went to the map and then back to his desk.

"I'm offering two hundred dollars in gold eagles to the man who helps me rescue Sadie. If the Indians want to make the arrangements to ransom her, the price is a hundred horses to the warrior."

The old prospector whistled. "Great damn! That's enough to make any brave change bands and be a rich man."

· "I just hope it works. How are your supplies, Mr. Thayer? Could you use some army hardtack, beans and salt pork? We have no tinned goods, but we'll set up your grub pack."

"That'd be more than welcome, Major," Thayer said with a twinkle in his eye. He always promoted these soldier boys at least one rank. They loved it.

"I'll have Corporal Swenson take care of you, Mr. Thayer. Stop by anytime. And remember those two hundred dollars. I want my little girl back."

The old prospector took Colt's offered hand with surprising grip and went out to see Cpl. Swenson who already was making out a list to go to the supply quartermaster.

Captain Harding stood on his small porch watching the prospector and the corporal heading for the quartermaster. He looked to the north. Sadie was up there somewhere!

Ten troopers rode by heading for the gate. He recognized them as members of his Lightning Company. They were going out to practice shooting under their mount's neck, Indian fashion. He would love to see the surprise on the Indian's faces when they found the cavalry attacking with some of the Comanche's own tricks and tactics.

He would use every strategy, every device, every method he could to defeat the Comanche. He was not too proud to use Comanche techniques. If they worked for the hostiles, they damn sure would work for a more disciplined unit. True, it had to be a tough, bone hard, mentally strong Cavalry outfit. But that's what the Lightning Company would be after another month of training.

By then the Comanche would be getting ready to go into their winter camps. Often several bands came together for the long winter, to gossip, trade lies, meet relatives separated during the summer and to pool their resources. He would love to catch two hundred braves hunkered down and feeling safe in some snow clogged small river valley and move in on them with every gun blazing!

Across the parade grounds Pamela Kenny smiled. It had been two days since the dinner at the Kenny's quarters, and Pamela hadn't seen Corporal Gregory since. So, she simply took matters in her own capable hands. Now she sat in the small A Company headquarters office as Victor Gregory sweated behind his desk.

"Miss Kenny, your father said he'd only be gone a few minutes. I'd appreciate it if you stay right there in the chair until he gets back. I worked three years to get my stripes. I ain't gonna risk losing them now for a kiss or two."

"Three or four or five warm, wonderful kisses, Victor. Wouldn't that feel good!" Pamela stood and walked with hips swaying and breasts bouncing as she moved up to him. She went around his desk. He stood suddenly. She pushed her chest against him and saw his nostrils flare and his breath catch.

Pamela pushed her hips hard against his and felt the bulge. He was excited, too!

Her arms went around him tightly. "Now kiss me proper or I won't let you go."

"Miss Kenny!"

"Call me Pamela, sweetheart. Now kiss me."

Victor hesitated, knew what it could cost him, but this feeling of wanting her so much was just as bad. He bent and kissed her. Tried to pull away but she held him. She nibbled at his lips, licked them with her tongue, then kissed him again so hard it made his teeth hurt.

Slowly she ground her hips against his. He was

getting bigger and bigger! Oh, yes!

The door opened and Captain Kenny stalked in. Cpl. Gregory jerked away and pushed at her, but her arms held him fast.

"Cpl. Gregory! Pamela! What in hell . . . ."

Captain Kenny charged across the room, pulled Pamela away and punched Cpl. Gregory in the mouth, slamming him backwards where he tripped over a chair and crashed to the floor. He looked up dazed and surprised.

"Keep your hands off my daughter, you little bastard!"

Pamela had been pushed to one side, now she went to Victor and helped him stand up, then turned toward her father.

"Daddy, you stop that! You touch him again and I'll report you to Captain Harding!" She walked around the small room a moment as she tried to hold onto her own temper. "Now everyone just calm down. It was just a little kiss, for goodness sakes. Daddy, don't tell me you never kissed a girl before you married mama."

"Young lady, I'll deal with you later. Now you get out of here, go home and stay in your room until I get there. You and I are going to have a long talk."

"Oh, Daddy. I know where babies come from and how they are made. I'm a grown woman!"

"Maybe in some ways. In other ways you're still a little girl. One thing for sure, you're still an unmarried young lady, and you'll get yourself straight home to your room. Now!"

"Oh. . . ."

"Not another word, Pamela Jean!"

When he used that tone and her middle name, he was near the point of exploding. She sighed, smiled at Cpl. Gregory, who stood ramrod stiffly at attention, and walked out the door.

"Damn!" Captain Kenny said. "At ease, Victor, relax. You're not in trouble, Pamela is. My daughter is spoiled and grew up without even asking me, and she's an outrageous flirt." Captain Kenny scowled.

He could be in trouble. It was a court martial offense for an officer to strike an enlisted man. He'd done so in front of a witness. Damn stupid of him. He had to tread delicately here.

"Corporal Gregory, my apologies to you. I shouldn't have struck you. It was a spur of the moment thing. I saw my little girl being assaulted by a man. Of course, now when I have a moment to think, I know that wasn't the case. I can see how she had you trapped. It's happened before, I'm afraid, on another post."

"I'm sorry, sir."

Kenny looked up in surprise. "I bet you don't mean that, Corporal. You mean you didn't enjoy getting kissed by my beautiful daughter?"

"It wasn't that, sir—I mean—I guess I did— but I didn't encourage. Oh, damn!"

Captain Kenny laughed now. The surprise of the tangle was over. He reasoned that the enlisted man would not report the blow to anyone. He was happy in his clerk's assignment so he was not in the field so much. Kenny was thankful that he'd come back when he did, before this romance situation got any more complicated. It was impossible. He was an enlisted. Not a chance he could marry a captain's daughter. The code just wouldn't allow it.

"Victor, don't worry about this situation. You're a good clerk, I'm not going to bust you for kissing my daughter. I'd also expect that you would understand my sudden fury when I caught her with you. That was why I struck out at you. For that I apologize."

"No apology needed, sir. It was still my fault. I should have pushed her away."

"Takes a strong man to do that to a pretty girl. I've had a problem or two like that when I was young." He walked around the small office. "Damn. I just wish it hadn't happened. Relax. I'll put this office off limits to my romantic little girl, and restrict her to her room for a week. That should help. Maybe by then she'll pick out somebody else to bedevil."

"Yes, sir. She sure is a right pretty girl."

"I know. The trouble is, she knows it, too. But we'll all survive until December. That's when she leaves for Austin and Boston. So, Corporal, is the little problem all forgotten? I'll forget you were kissing my daughter, and you'll forget that my fist somehow grazed your jaw."

"Yes, sir, that seems like a good trade."

Captain Kenny held out his hand and they shook.

"Now, Corporal, let's look over that list of weapons. We've got to get men in the same squad with the same type of rifle, or at least the same size of ammunition. We'll trade around within the company as much as we can. We may need to make some trades with other companies as well."

The next day Captain Kenny led twenty of his men on a scouting patrol. He had been assigned to it a week before. They would be gone for three days and two nights. Sgt. Zach Upland would remain at the fort in charge of the rest of the company and the company clerk would remain behind as well for administration.

It was a routine patrol, a way of showing the flag to the hostiles if they were in the area, to remind them that the U.S. Cavalry was on duty and would challenge them.

The first day of the patrol, Cpl. Gregory winced each time the door opened to his small A Company office, but he was relieved at the end of the day when Pamela had not come in. She was supposed to be restricted to her room. But he figured Pamela would work some dodge to get around that.

Gregory was from Iowa, had been working on his father's farm until one day he decided he had been looking at the rear end of a plow mule long enough. He enlisted. He had been in his share of Indian fights, came in just at the end of the fighting in Sixty-five so missed the Civil War.

Now he was concentrating on getting into a position where he could strike for his sergeant's stripes. Once he got them he was set up for the rest of his life in the army. A sergeant had the best spot in the Cavalry!

The second day went by without incident as well. He and Sgt. Zach Upland kept the company going on an even keel with some extra duty for those left behind.

He had to get the roster set for the next day and before Cpl. Gregory realized it, the afternoon was gone. He lit a lamp to take care of the last page he had to check.

He was concentrating on the papers and didn't even look up when the door opened and closed.

"Yeah?" he asked.

When no one responded, he looked up to find Pamela Kenny a foot from his face. She kissed him at once, sitting in his lap on the chair, pulling his face up to hers.

"No!" he said forcefully when he tugged his lips away. "Your dad would kill us both. Stop it!"

"Victor, you don't mean that. I've wanted to kiss you again for just days and days!" She kissed him quickly and this time he couldn't protest. He had thought of her every waking moment, but knew she was unattainable. She was officer people.

When she let his lips go, she nuzzled against him.

"We can't do this. You know the army rules about enlisted and officers. You're an officer's daughter. I'd get rawhided out of here on a rail, I touch you."

"I won't let them." She stood, caught his hand and pulled him toward the outside door. She pushed the locking bolt in firmly, then led him to the small back room, the captain's office. She left the door open so some of the lamp light would come into the room, then she kissed him again, pressing her sleek body against him from toe to chest.

He growled and put his arms around her pulling her tighter against him.

When the kiss broke at last she pushed away slightly and began unbuttoning the four fasteners on the top of her dress. It snuggled against her chin and came to her wrists and swept the floor as most dresses did.

He watched with fascination. Then she spread the top of the dress wide and to his surprise there was no other garments under it. Her breasts glowed, pink and white, erect red nipples pulsating as he watched them.

Victor Gregory had never been with a woman before. She lifted his hands to her breasts and held them there. Then she kissed him tenderly and they sat down on the rough boards of the floor.

Her hands rubbed his crotch, then fumbled at the buttons.

"Darling Vic, don't worry. I'll show you exactly what to do. No one will come. Father is gone for another day, and I told Mother I wanted to talk to Mrs. Edwards. We have two hours to love each other!"

Quickly she wiggled out of her clothes until she was naked, then she pulled off his clothes.

He sat there staring at her completely nude form. He had never seen a woman like that before. She was better than any of his sexy dreams. He reached for her and soon discovered that making love was not as hard as he thought it might be.

Three times they brought each other to the heights and Vic Gregory could never remember being so delighted, so thrilled, so much in love.

As they pulled on their clothes, he was full of plans.

"My enlistment is up in two months. I was going to reenlist, but I don't have to. My dad needs help with the farm back in Iowa. It's plenty big enough for two families. We'll get married here, of course, or in Austin. I'll be a civilian again."

She kissed him and let him pet her again, then they slipped into the other room.

"Darling Victor, don't make a lot of plans. Things can change. Let's just enjoy what we have now, and see what happens." She kissed him, then brazenly rubbed his crotch. He reached for her hungrily, but she pushed him away and stepped into the night. She was full of talk about Mrs. Edwards when she got back to her quarters. Her mother was working on piecing a quilt, and barely noticed when Pamela came in.

The next morning, after their three days of practice, Lightning Company assembled in the sandy draw and stacked up four cardboard boxes so they were about the size of a man. They anchored the bottom box with heavy rocks, and wired them together so they would stay upright.

Captain Harding watched as the squads came past on their shooting test. He had the fourth squad lead out. The first two men had learned their lesson well. Most of the men wrapped one leg around the saddlehorn, leaned down and with both hands fired their Spencers under the horse's neck. They were each allowed two shots.

After each man passed the target, markers ran in and circled any holes in the "man" sized cardboard boxes and called out the hits. There was a drawn bullseye on the "chest" of the boxes. A chest hit counted five points, a hit anywhere else counted one.

Only one man fell off his mount during the test. He was given three hours extra riding training to perfect his under-neck firing.

Captain Harding looked at the results that Cpl. Swenson had tallied.

Three men in each of the squads had scored one or more chest hits. The top point producer was the second squad which had six chest hits and eight other hits for a total of thirty-eight points.

Captain Harding nodded. "Well done, men. Now when the chance comes, we can give the bloody Comanche nobody to shoot at the way they do to us."

Next on the training were ambush attacks. Captain Harding led the men in a march through the prairie in the usual four abreast formation, then suddenly he would pull one of his ivory handled pistols and fire twice in the air.

"Ambush! From the left," he shouted. "Dismount and take cover!"

At once the men dismounted, one tropper in each squad was assigned the job of leading the horses away to safety and protecting them. The rest of the men flattened behind any cover they could find, and on a given signal began firing their allotted four rounds to the left.

Captain Harding sat above it all with his pocket-watch out watching the second hand tick around. He noted times as the horses were led away, the men found protection, and the command by Sgt. Casemore to fire was given.

Four times they went through the exercise, then Captain Harding led them back to Fort Comfort. He decided there was enough heat in the sun to dry another series of adobe bricks, and assigned C Company the next day to go to the draw with the exposed adobe clay deposits and make one hundred adobe blocks.

Their own masons would lay up the blocks when they were dry. He had forgotten about working on the rest of the fort. Now he knew it was time. Soon the snow would be flying.

Back at the fort, he sat in his office chair and stared out the small window for a moment. His Lightning Company was progressing nicely. He wished he had some kind of cold weather gear for the men. If he took them out into three foot deep snow in their standard blue uniforms half of them would freeze to death.

He would write to San Antonio about what equipment he could requisition for winter patrols. He didn't think he would have any problems getting what they had. The real worry was that the army had little equipment for the really cold winter weather.

His eyes strayed across the map of West Texas. No one had been by the fort since Mr. Thayer, the prospector. Someone must be out there in the Comanche country. Soon, perhaps soon there would be a break.

7

The next morning, Captain Harding was in the middle of a letter to San Antonio headquarters asking what cold weather gear the army had developed for winter patrolling.

Cpl. Swenson knocked and came into his office.

"Sir, there's a man outside who says he knows where Sadie was ten days ago."

"Bring him in!" Colt snapped, jumping to his feet, the letter forgotten. He was almost to the door when the man came in. He looked more Indian than white. He had long black hair, coppery skin, a hawk nose and he wore buckskin with fringes more common in the mountains of the far West. Dark eyes took in the office in a sweeping glance, then settled on Colt.

"Captain Harding," he said formally. "My name is Wesley Tallpine. I know where White Eagle's tipis were ten days ago. Your daughter is with him."

Harding stepped forward, held out his hand. The man took it and shook. His face was blank, unreadable.

"I hope to God you do, Wesley Tallpine. I'm Colt Harding. Are you sure it was my daughter?"

"Can't be absolutely sure. But they called her Laughing Golden Hair. She was four, maybe five years old. She has been adopted by a woman called Cries In The Morning. Both live in White Eagle's big tent with an Eagle head painted on the side."

"I've seen the tipi up on the Wichita," Colt said.

"They're near that now, on part of what I think is Croton Creek, that runs into the Wichita. To hell and gone up there, Captain."

"Two hundred miles?"

"Closer to two hundred and twenty. Lost my trading wagon first day out from there. Left me with my riding horse and I came down here in ten days, easy twenty mile a day."

"Excuse me, Mr. Tallpine, but are you Indian?"

"Most folks don't wait so long, Captain. They just call me Breed and have it done. My mother is white, my father is Comanche. I was the result of a raid on a white settlement where I was later born. But I also know the Comanche lingo and the people. Lived with Trailing Bear's band for three years. I can also read and write."

"Good man to have around. The girl was brown-eyed, right?"

"No, sir, Captain. Eyes blue like a mountain lake in morning."

"You're sure it was Walking White Eagle's band?"

"I sold him some goods. Curious, he paid for them in gold double eagles. Never seen a Comanche do that before."

"Curious is right. Will you lead me back to his

camp?"

"The two hundred still waiting?"

"In gold, as soon as we get little Sadie out of there."

Tallpine hesitated. "Can't right guarantee you'll get her out. Comanches don't like giving up adopted children. I'll guarantee to guide you to the camp for a hundred dollars."

"Done!" Colt thundered holding out his hand. Wesley took it and grinned.

"See the quartermaster for some dinner and gear if you'll need any. Is your horse good? We'll be covering sixty to sixty-five miles a day. Show him to Corporal Swenson. We'll be leaving at five-thirty A.M. We travel hard and fast, no wagons."

"I'll be damned. Sixty-five miles? I figured you'd do sixteen maybe eighteen."

"Not with this kind of information." He led Tallpine to the outer office.

"Swenson, get Sergeant Casemore in here on the double. We'll be leaving on a patrol early in the morning. Take care of Mr. Tallpine here, the best we have to offer. Send Casemore in when he arrives."

Captain Harding went back into his office and studied his map of Texas. They would be traveling almost due north past a sometimes camp ground the Comanche used to use. Then on north to the very edge of the caprock below the Staked Plains. They would not be quite as far north as when they whipped White Eagle before, but they would be farther west.

Harding had no thoughts that this would be a simple walk up attack. He was sure that after his lesson, White Eagle would have seasoned warriors out about three deep as lookouts and scouts to protect his south and west flanks. The band might have left and be in a hunting camp. If so the Tonkawas could track them. An attack during a hunt would be to the Pony Soldier's advantage.

Colt went to a corner wooden file case bolted to the floor and unlocked the bottom drawer. He took the drawer all the way out. Below it was a floor safe dug through a hole in the boards and into the dry Texas soil.

After working a combination, Colt opened the lid and took out a thick leather bag with a draw-string. From it he counted out five double eagle gold coins. He closed the bag and put it back.

Five minutes later Sgt. Casemore stopped in front of his desk and saluted.

"Sergeant Casemore reporting as ordered, sir!"

"At ease, Casemore. Let's look at the map." The two men went to the large scale wall map. "We're here in Fort Comfort. Tomorrow morning we leave for a ride north, about two hundred and twenty miles. Four days of riding. We attack the next day. A man came in with positive identification on Sadie. She's with White Eagle, for sure."

"We're ready sir. The usual double ration of ammunition?"

Colt nodded.

"Rations for what, four days, and Tonkawa meat for the rest, Captain?"

"Sounds good. Have your men get their gear ready and get them bedded down as soon as it gets dark. We'll move out at five-thirty A.M."

"Yes, sir!"

When Cpl. Swenson came in to tell him the trader was being fed and would bunk down in the barracks, Captain Harding told his clerk to notify six Tonkawa scouts they would be needed for a patrol.

"Have the top six men we usually take. We'll use four as scouts instead of two, and two for hunters."

"Yes, sir."

The first day on the trail was uneventful. The Tonkawa scouts brought down a two point buck deer the first afternoon and they roasted venison as soon as they stopped for the night. They had covered sixty miles, Colt figured.

He chewed through the seared part of a section of ribs and tore off the juicy venison underneath. It wasn't a neat way to eat but the mule deer meat was delicious. As soon as they ate, the tired men fell into their blankets.

The second day went about the same, but no big hunting success. Three rabbits and a pair of ducks. Colt passed and ate hardtack and drank his coffee.

By the end of the fourth day they had covered another 200 miles. They had slowed down when the scouts reported some signal fires ahead. Whenever possible they traveled through draws and valleys and in woodsy fringes along streams.

But now and then there was an expanse of open country they had to cross.

The Tonkawa soon read the smokes.

"They know we come," War Hatchet, the head Tonkawa scout, said after riding back from the point a mile ahead. "Smoke say forty Pony Soldiers."

"Damn. There goes our surprise. How far ahead of us is the camp, Tallpine?"

The Breed stared at the darkening country

around him. "Not more than five miles," he said.

"Will the Comanche move their camp?" Captain Harding asked the Tonkawa.

"Yes, no?" he asked.

Tallpine shook his head. "No, White Eagle won't move. By now he knows how fast we're traveling. He knows we could run him down with the heavy travois and the women and kids. He'll find a defensive spot and fight. He'll also try to ambush us as we move up."

When the men had eaten and rested for an hour, Colt called them out of their blankets.

"We'll move up to within rifle range of them in the darkness," Colt ordered. "That will spoil any surprises they have planned for us tomorrow morning."

Tallpine grinned. "You would make a good Comanche chief," the halfbreed trader said.

The scouts pulled back to a hundred yards and the men walked their mounts forward silently. Nothing jangled, there was no talk, only the soft walking hoofbeats and the occasional blow of the army geldings.

They moved a mile with no problems. Then an owl hooted in front of them, and War Hatchet appeared out of the gloom beside Colt.

"Not owl, Comanche," War Hatchet said softly.

Tallpine agreed. "Damn poor owl call," he said. "Sounds like a boy."

Another mile forward a better owl called into the night. It was answered by a call farther ahead. Colt grinned. The Comanches knew forty Pony Soldiers were moving up through the night toward their camp. They had no way of knowing when an attack might come. The Comanche warriors would be awake all night waiting. Colt would let his men get some sleep when they were closer.

There were no more owl calls.

"The Comanche scouts know we're here," Tall-pine told Captain Harding. "They will follow us as far as we go, and report to White Eagle."

"So no one surprises anyone else," Colt said. "It will be a matter of who can fight the best."

"And who has the best rifles," Tallpine said.

Colt looked at him in the dim moonlight.

"Rifles? White Eagle has rifles?"

"He had them when you attacked him before, you told me. When I was in his camp, I saw several warriors with rifles. They seemed to know how to use them."

"He steals them from everywhere that he raids. He picked up twelve rifles and twelve pistols when he attacked our supply train four months ago."

The scouts came back and halted the troop. They reported they wanted to work forward carefully and check the lay of the hills just this side of the camp.

An hour later War Hatchet came back and motioned them forward. They walked their animals, still in a column of fours, for two more miles, then dismounted, left them in control of the designated wrangler for each squad, and moved forward on foot.

They went up a rolling hill, through light brush and stunted live oaks. At the top of the hill they stopped. They were less than a hundred feet above a silvery strip of a river below them some three hundred yards away.

In the moonlight they could see the tops of the

tipis where they were pitched protected by a twenty foot deep gorge the stream had cut through the land.

They would not be able to fire directly into the camp or the tipis. Colt frowned.

"Didn't seem this protected when I was down in there," Tallpine said. "But then I came in from the other way."

"Too damn late to come at them from the north!" Colt brayed.

He sat down and stared at the tops of the tipis. Too late to go around. The other side might be equally protected. The hostiles knew they were here and had not attacked them. They must feel their camp was well protected. And the damn savages had a good supply of rifles and probably plenty of stolen ammunition.

Colt listened to a night hawk, the shrill cry of the bird as it made a kill. He doubted if that was an Indian. He tried to think how he would defend the gorge if he occupied it.

He would cut notches in the edge of the cliff and put his riflemen there with a foot high parapet of earth to fire over. He would have an excellent field of fire up the hill aimed at anyone attempting to come over the top. A brutal advantage.

He needed a five inch gun to blast those snipers off the hill and to drop exploding rounds into the gorge.

Next best thing were the hand bombs he had prepared for an attack several months ago but did not have a chance to use. They were dynamite sticks cut in half, taped together along with thirty to fifty large headed roofing nails. The nails were taped tightly to the dynamite. When the dynamite exploded the short nails screamed out in all directions like deadly shrapnel. He had brought tabout twenty of the bombs which were distributed through the troop.

Tomorrow he could send two men to crawl down the hill with rifle fire protection and get close enough to lob the bombs into the village.

No! One of the bombs could kill Sadie!

He would be limited in using the bombs against the snipers along the rim, if indeed White Eagle put men there.

Colt moved below the ridgeline on the reverse slope and lit a match to check the time. Three A.M.

A night attack!

That would let his men work down the three hundred yards to the edge of the gorge under protection of darkness. Even if the Redskins had rifles at the lip of the gorge, the shooters would have no targets!

He alerted the men, told Sgt. Casemore and the squad leader his plans.

"We'll work down to the lip of the gorge as silently as possible. None of the hand bombs will be thrown without my explicit permission. My daughter is down there. Her safety is my primary concern.

"No one is permitted to fire at or near the tallest tipi with the eagle head painted on it. We move out in five minutes. Absolute silence and no firing until I give the command."

The troopers spread out at five yard intervals and moved down the slope on whispered command. Halfway down the night hawk screamed in protest, and Colt knew then that it was not a hawk but a Comanche within fifty feet of them, pacing them to the side. He sent two

Tonkawas that direction and a few minutes later heard a scream.

One less Comanche.

They made it to the lip of the gorge and looked over. None of the troopers found any firing positions on the lip. They looked down at the campsite and saw that everything appeared normal.

No people were in evidence, but there would be none this time of the night.

Tallpine edged up to Captain Harding.

"There should be some smoke from the tipis," he whispered. Some banked fires. My guess is the camp is deserted, that there is not a Comanche there. They have scattered across the hills to the far side, and down the gorge both ways."

Captain Harding looked over the situation. He sent one squad back to the top of the hill and told them to dig in on the reverse slope to give them covering fire. He put two men on each side to cover their flanks. Then he passed the word that the men should find cover from the slope across the way. The other side of the gorge was little more than fifty yards away.

One small, folding shovel had been issued to each squad, and now the men used the tool, their bayonets, and carried larger rocks to build protection from direct fire across the gorge. An hour later the activity was over and the troopers settled down to wait for daylight.

Captain Harding talked with Tallpine. "What will White Eagle do when it's light?"

Tallpine looked at the situation. He had quickly brought up rocks and fashioned protection for himself and Captain Harding.

"White Eagle will look over the situation. If he

thinks he can attack and win, he will. He has protected his women and children and the old men. He will provide rifles to protect the tipis. There will be no chance to burn them this time. They will storm back in a direct battle to protect their tipis. Without them they all would die this winter."

"We can throw our hand bombs into the tipis, damage them as much as possible," Captain Harding said.

"This is not the camp site where the tipis were when I was here before," Tallpine said. "I knew it was different. White Eagle must have been moving from one spot to another to find the perfect site that he could protect."

"When did he take his women and children out?" Colt asked.

"Probably when his scouts reported that you were moving forward under darkness to get into position to attack the village. He had no choice then."

Each squad appointed a guard and the rest dozed. They got two hours of sleep before daylight.

With the first streaks of dawn, Colt Harding was alert and watchful. There had been no sounds, no movement from the village below. Not a horse, not a dog was present. It indeed was deserted by its people.

Captain Harding scanned the edge of the ravine on the far side. It slanted upward slightly as the land did on this side, but he could find no sign of new earth moved, no feathers, no lances, no Indians.

An owl hooted across the ravine, then one far to the right.

Tallpine came awake at once. "The Comanche are ready to attack us," he said softly.

Captain Harding passed the word to his right and left. "Alert. Be ready. Do not fire without my command."

Down the line a trooper hunched up to change position, lifting his backside a foot above his parapet.

A rifle snarled from across the gorge, the round burning a quarter inch gouge out of the trooper's rear end, dropping him into his hole with a screech.

"Two rounds per rifle. Fire!" Captain Harding bellowed. Sixty rounds of hot lead drilled across the gorge into every shrub, rock and hump that might be providing concealment for a Comanche.

When the sound died down, Colt checked the village below. It strung out a quarter of a mile along the gorge, but still he saw no Comanches. He took one of the hand bombs from his shoulder bag, checked the four inch dynamite fuse and made sure the detonator was pressed securely into the dynamite.

He lit the fuse and when he was sure it was burning well, threw it over the side toward the closet tipi, maybe thirty yards away across the small stream and fifty feet below.

The bomb landed three feet short of the tipi, jolted forward another foot, then exploded with a shattering roar that echoed up and down the gorge. The nails slashed through the tipi, gouging holes a foot long in places, snarling through a small hole in others.

When the sound quieted, Colt turned to the left, then the right, at last he looked up the hill. There was a flurry of rifle fire from the top aimed the other way. Sgt. Casemore was more than earning his keep. The Comanches had tried a rear attack.

Captain Harding passed the word for the grenadiers in each squad to throw two hand bombs each. Soon the eight bombs sailed into the air, blasting in and among the tipis below. One of the buffalo skin covered tipis burst into flames and burned brightly in the soft morning light. Half a dozen others were riddled by the roofing nail shrapnel.

The answer came from across the gorge at once. A shower of fifty arrows arched into the sky so they would fall on the dug in troopers as artillery shells would.

A pair of screeches down the line gave evidence that some of the arrows had cut white flesh.

To the left flank a rifle fired once, then again and again.

Another probe.

Captain Harding motioned to Tallpine. "Call to White Eagle. Tell him if he sends out Laughing Golden Hair, his band may live in peace without the Pony Soldiers hounding them."

The halfbreed called out the message in Comanche, and waited for a reply. It came a moment later.

"White eyes attack Comanche. Comanche lives in peace. Pony Soldiers must leave."

"Tell him we will not leave without the small golden haired girl," Captain Harding said.

The message was called across the gap.

"We have only our own children. You must leave now."

"Tell him if he does not give up Laughing Golden Hair, a thousand Pony Soldiers will come and overwhelm him, and kill everyone in his band,

and destroy his tipis and his winter food supply and the name of White Eagle will be known throughout the Comanche nation as a fool who died and let his whole band die as well because he was stupid and without honor and because he refused to let a captured white girl go free.''

It was a long speech, and when he finished, Tallpine lifted his brows.

"Now you've made him mad,'' the Breed predicted.

White Eagle shouted back at once and Tallpine translated.

"White Eagle and his band can defend themselves. But they will not kill all of the Pony Soldiers if they leave at once and never return. If they don't there is no way they will live to see another sunrise.''

Captain Harding replied: "If White Eagle does not give up Laughing Golden Hair, two thousand Pony Soldiers will track his band forever, and punish them and pursue them all the way west to the smoking waters and north to the Big Muddy. The White Eagle band will never know a day of peace again!''

White Eagle replied: "If the Pony Soldiers don't leave before the sun is at the top of the sky, he will deliver Laughing Golden Hair to the Pony Soldiers fort one pound at a time until the Pony Soldier captain has all of the child in a hundred pieces. The blue shirts must go, or the small girl will die when the sun is on top of the sky.''

Tallpine translated it quickly as it was spoken. When the last words were given he nodded to Colt.

"I'd say we go. Chiefs do this all the time, use hostages and captives as poker chips. Captives have no value to a chief. And shouting this threat to you, so all his people could hear it, means he must carry out the threat or lose much of his good medicine and his power to lead his people."

Colt stared at the other side of the gully for a full minute, then nodded. "Pass the word. Squad one move up the hill smartly, the other two squads be ready with covering fire if the enemy fires. Go!"

They got all three squads up the hill without a shot being fired. Sgt. Casemore called in the flankers and they waited for the next command.

Captain Harding watched the Indians across the way move skillfully back out of the line of fire into pecan and live oak trees across the way. They had won again. Damnit!

He nodded to Sgt. Casemore and motioned to move back toward the horses. The men tending the mounts had taken the usual precautions but walked the animals forward as close to the troops as was safe.

Ten minutes later, Captain Harding and his forty men with only three slightly wounded, moved down the valley to the south, heading back to the fort. It would be a long ride home, and an uhappy one.

Colt Harding stared back at the hilltop again. There had to be a way to get Sadie back from that savage, but how? He had to devise a plan that would not fail. He had to rescue Sadie before the Comanches turned her into a savage!

8

Half a dozen Comanche warriors followed the march of Lightning Company as it headed home. When the troop was ten miles south of the Indian camp, all but two Indian lookouts went back to Croton Creek to spread the word. Only a few warriors had returned to the campsite to check on the damage.

The bombs the Pony Soldiers had thrown caused severe damage. It would take many hours of splicing and patching by the women to get the tipi covers back in shape for the winter cold.

When the scout braves returned, the call was given and from everywhere around the village the People appeared and returned to their tipis. The fire started by one of the bombs had burned only one tipi. It was a total loss. At once new skins were given to the Elk Wound family so a new cover could be made.

Always Smiling went into the woods to find strong poles to form the tipi frame. They were hard to find in this area. She wished they were in the fringes of a pine forest. It took her the rest of the day and then she found only three of the seven needed.

Warrior's Woman had begun the task of laying out the skins, matching and shifting and then cutting them to fit to form the cover. It was all done on a clear spot on the ground near the stream. When Warrior's Woman had each section ready, she waved and three or four women came in and stitched the heavy pieces of buffalo hide together with tough buffalo sinew.

The women worked until darkness, then went to their own lodges to cook food and do the rest of their daily chores.

For an hour after they got back to camp a search was made. At last the warriors had found Rabbit Lair. He had been one of the scouts shadowing the Pony Soldiers when they arrived last night. Even before his body came back to camp over his war pony, the wailing and keening came from the whole village.

They had suffered their last loss in several months, but it made it no easier for Rabbit Lair's family. He would be prepared and then properly buried sitting upright in the highest peak they could find among the low hills.

There his spirit would be free to soar into the sky and to fly with the eagles and to reach the great hunting grounds where every shot was sure and every stomach was full.

Sadie did not know of the attack until she returned from a long horseback ride with her mother. The two had been instructed by White Eagle to go upstream, a two hour ride, and stay over night. That had been when it was still light the previous evening. White Eagle knew the Pony Soldiers were coming. He would take no chances of them finding Laughing Golden Hair.

Sadie had enjoyed the ride, eating a new kind of blueberry, and playing in the stream. Then they slept on the side of a hill under a huge live oak tree. It was like an overnight picnic!

Cries In The Morning did not tell her about the Pony Soldiers. She had taken Sadie three hours upstream rather than two just to be sure. When they came back that morning it had been slowly, carefully, watching every direction. When she heard the faint call of the cry that the enemy had been defeated and it was now safe, Cries In The Morning smiled and hurried with Laughing Golden Hair to White Eagle's tipi.

By that time Talks A Lot had repaired most of the damage in the big tipi with the eagle painted on the side. The worst of the bomb explosion had missed the chief's tent. It had two slashes and two of the nails had punched through the hides with their points but been stopped by the flat heads.

The strange nails were pulled out and saved.

"Soldiers here?" Sadie asked her mother.

Cries In The Morning nodded. "*Toquet*," all is well. She explained that they had come and thew bombs but then White Eagle talked them into going back to their house of many walls.

"Why did they come?" Sadie asked.

"Who knows what the *tosi-tivo* think or why they do it. They came but they are gone. That is good. See if you can find some wild onions for me along the creek."

Sadie and two small friends hunted for wild onions, found one small patch and dug up half of them, leaving the rest for whoever found them the next day and so they would grow and multiply in Mother Earth.

The talk was only of the raid, and how they had outsmarted the Pony Soldiers. The women chattered while they repaired the tipis and sewed on the new one. The warriors gathered in small groups talking about the raid, and how they could have performed better.

White Eagle sat in his tipi with the flap closed staring into a small fire and smoking his pipe which he had filled with fresh tobacco from the trader.

He was troubled more than he would say. How had the voice speaking in the People's language known the name of Laughing Golden Hair? How had the Pony Soldiers come directly to the Comanche camp even in the dead of night?

There were a dozen hard questions for which he had no answers. There was no one to ask. His people looked to him for answers, not to bring him answers. There were no old men he could talk to.

Runs Plenty was so old his mind wandered. If he was still not the best arrow maker among the Comanches, he would have been left behind to push his nose into the dust and die with dignity. Two other former members of the council had lost all interest in the band, or how it functioned. All they wanted was a pipe and one good meal a day. They rocked their days away sitting in the sun and making up lies about their youth.

Captain Two Pistols had found him again. How could White Eagle fight against this Pony Soldier? Some of the warriors wanted to track the Pony Soldiers, catch them in the open and attack, holding them there until their bullets ran out, then cut them into small pieces and bring back many guns and scalps.

But this Captain Two Pistols was too smart for that. He would never wait for them to catch him. His men could ride as far a day as the best Comanche pony could. It would be hard to catch them before they found their fort.

An hour after sunset, the twelve members of the council sat around a small fire where the shadows bounced off the thick wall behind them, and the stream chattered at their feet. At the council each of the members could talk, no one outranked anyone else.

"I was sad when we let the Pony Soldiers walk away without a fight," Running Thunder said. "We should have attacked, followed them, chased them all the way back to their little fort."

"And we would have lost a dozen warriors!" another man said. "We stopped the white eye's attack. We turned him back, we defeated him, and at the cost of only one warrior. It was a great victory for Comanche warriors!"

"No!" Fox Paw bellowed. The young warrior was only nineteen, but already one of the best in the band. "We were like old women. We did not fight, we defended. We were not warriors; we were rocks stopping bullets from the puny rifles. A Comanche lives to fight, to make war on the Pony Soldiers."

He stopped and looked around and saw enough nods to encourage him.

"We should fight the Pony Soldier whenever we find him, and especially when he chases us down to our own village. Such a thing must never happen again! We had six hours warning that the Pony Soldiers were coming. Six hours of daylight. We could have dropped our tipis and scattered in twenty different directions and left the Pony Soldiers chasing their own horses' tails!''

"The council decided we should stand and confront the Pony Soldiers with our camp so easy to defend," White Eagle said. "Where was Fox Paw when the council decided? He was sitting with the pipe in his hand. Will he not now take the responsibility of his own decisions?"

"In my heart I protested the plan even as I accepted it," Fox Paw said.

"My ears can't hear what your heart says unless your heart uses your mouth to tell me," Elk Wound said. "We have council so we may speak our hearts and our minds."

"Captain Two Guns must be punished!" Fox Paw shouted. "We must seek him out and slaughter his troops and take his scalp as a warning to all other Pony Soldiers!"

"Fox Paw demonstrates his nineteen years of lack of wisdom," White Eagle said softly. "To seek out a Pony Soldier captain is to ride into his fort. The Captain Two Guns can bring four times as many riders as he had today. He can bring as many guns as we have horses and ponies. We must think clearly, talk straight, and decide where to move now that the Pony Soldiers know where we are."

"We should move toward the Pony Soldier fort so we may launch a raid on it," Fox Paw screeched.

The council was still for a moment.

"We should move north, past the Peace River, high on the tributaries of the Red, perhaps to Mulberry Creek where we made camp one summer," Thunder Dog said. "A hundred miles to the north, but still in front of the caprock."

"I will not run away from Captain Two Guns!" Fox Paw thundered. He jumped up, his feet spread wide, his hand on the knife at his hip where it hung from his surcingle. "I am not afraid of the Captain Two Guns!"

"We must stand and fight somewhere," Proud Buck said softly. He was old, nearly fifty. "We have been driven back and back from our lands. We must stand and fight somewhere or we will be forced up to the Staked Plains and then off the far side of that."

White Eagle stood and walked around the fire. He turned at the far side and faced the council.

"We are Comanche. Many bands are moving. We can not battle the whole two thousand Pony Soldiers alone. There are ten times two thousand of the white eye soldiers. Not even all of the Comanche bands together can battle a forest of white eyes like that."

He went back to his place around the fire and sat.

"Some of the old ways are fading away. The white eyes are limiting us in some areas. It is like trying to push against the spring flood of a mighty river. We will never win. But we can live as the Comanche always has, for as long as possible. We can promote the old ways, we can move and hunt and winter and be Comanche to the very last. It would be foolish to throw ourselves into the whistling bombs and the long guns of two thousand white eye Pony Soldiers."

He loked around the council. Fox Paw still stood defiantly.

"It is my suggestion that we move north, as Thunder Dog suggested. We may go all the way to Mulberry Creek. Always Smiling will find a good camp. What is the feeling of the members of the council?"

"Wait!" Fox Paw moved closer to the council members. "It was easy to see today that White Eagle is protecting the band, but he is spending more time to protect the one who is causing us the trouble. Without the white eye girl, Laughing Golden Hair, we would not be Captain Two Guns' target. He is not after us. He is searching for his child. We spend too much time worrying about her safety rather than that of the band as a whole."

"Let each man speak his heart and his mouth," White Eagle said.

Each warrior talked briefly about his feelings about moving, when White Eagle lit the pipe and it went around. Each man smoked it except Fox Paw. He was free to move with the band or not. Each Comanche could go his own way whenever he wanted to.

They would move in two days. It gave everyone time enough to do things in an efficient organized way. They had a few more racks of meat to get dried, the packs to make.

The next morning, just as the sun came up, Fox Paw waited outside White Eagle's tipi. He wore only his breechclout and moccasins. In his right hand he carried his knife. In the left a three-foot-long piece of rawhide two inches wide.

Two warriors going to train their war ponies passed and spoke to him, but he ignored them, staring at the still closed flap of White Eagle's tent.

A half hour later the flap came open and White Eagle stepped outside. He saw Fox Paw, saw the knife, saw the stripe of rawhide. White Eagle sighed. "Fox Paw, there is no need for this."

"I have a need. The whole band has a need. We have a great need for a new leader."

"Is he to be only a boy such as you, Fox Paw?"

Anger flared in the youth's face. "I am a Comanche warrior. I have made coup many times. My scalp pole is as full as any warrior in our camp, as full as your own."

"Still, you are only a boy. Take your young family. Go with no anger, find a band that fits your beliefs, your temperament."

"No. I like this band. I just don't like its leader." He threw down the strip of rawhide at White Eagle's feet.

"You don't have to do this, Fox Paw. Your pride is hurt. Forget it. Take your family and find a new band."

"Pick up the fighting rawhide!" Fox Paw screamed. By then half a dozen braves had gathered. Women and children peeked out through tipi flaps.

"There is no other way, Fox Paw?"

"None. Soon you will be the ex-leader of this band!"

White Eagle bent and picked up the rawhide strip. He looked at it for a moment, then glanced at Fox Paw. "When?"

"When the sun is at the top of the sky. At the ceremonial fire."

"I'll be there."

Word spread through the camp like a prairie fire. Seldom did a dispute between members of a band become so heated that it could not be talked out by the old men or at least by the war leader. Now and then it happened that neither of the parties would leave the band. If the problem was serious enough it could be settled only with a *muerto* strip of rawhide.

As White Eagle sat in his lodge preparing himself for the fight, he could remember seeing only one *muerto* fight before. One of the warriors had been killed, and the other one so badly cut up that he never rode into battle again.

White Eagle seriously considered packing his tipi and leaving the band. He knew that almost all of the fifty tipis would also come down and go with him. But that would not settle the problem.

Fox Paw was young, strong, agile. White Eagle knew that he faced the reality that he could be dead before nightfall. He took a deep breath and looked around the tipi. It had been a good life. He had tasted leadership, victory, a good woman, he had seen his children born, he had defeated the Pony Soldiers. It was a good day to die.

Every activity stopped in the village as the sun climbed to the highest point in the sky. Fox Paw waited at the ceremonial fire ring. The council sat in its place minus two members. Everyone in the camp who could walk there, sat or stood around a large circle that had been drawn on the bare earth.

White Eagle walked through the group looking at no one. When he saw Fox Paw he riveted his stare on the young warrior. White Eagle carried the *muerto* strip of rawhide. Sometimes a knot was fashioned in each end, but not this time.

He walked to within six feet of Fox Paw. White Eagle looked up at the sun.

"It is time," the eldest in the council said.

White Eagle threw the strip of rawhide at Fox Paw's feet. His sullen expression changed to a smile. He grabbed the rawhide and held one end, walked up to White Eagle and handed him the other end.

Thunder Dog stood from his position in the council and nodded to each of the men. They took the rawhide strip and each man put one end of it in his mouth. White teeth clamped down hard on the strip.

The rawhide strip had to remain in the mouths of both men. That was the only rule. If one man dropped the strip—he lost—he died.

The men faced each other. Each had his favorite fighting knife. Both of these were about twelve inches overall, with an eight inch blade that would cut on either side of the three inch tip.

They each wore only their breechclout and moccasins.

Thunder Dog lifted a lance and held it. The two fighters watched him. Then suddenly he hurled the lance into the ground beside his feet and the fight began.

When the three foot strip of rawhide was taut, only the tips of the fighting knives could reach the other man. But when they surged together all parts of the other man's body were open to attack.

The two men crouched, knees bent, arms wide for balance and attack. Both men were experts at knife fighting. They held the knives the way one would a saber to slash or stab. Slowly they circled each other, the rawhide tight.

Fox Paw jolted inward, his left hand out to ward off any blow at a vital area, his own knife thrusting forward at White Eagle's chest. White Eagle was slightly taller than the other man. He lunged to one side to avoid the blow, pulling Fox Paw with him on the leash.

White Eagle's knife slashed out at the unprotected left arm, and drew a quarter of an inch deep blood line three inches long.

Fox Paw pulled back and they feinted and circled.

Both men tried to be patient. The strategy in any kind of knife fight, White Eagle knew, was to be patient and wait for an opening. If you had to attack, be sure that you had a hand or shoulder to take a minor cut or stab as a sacrifice to get inside the opponent's blade and give him a deadly wound.

There were no rules. Kicking, biting, hitting, anything was allowed when a man fought for his life!

The two circled each other again, then White Eagle dodged to one side, reversed himself and slashed out with his knife in a roundhouse swing of his right arm. The sudden tactic caught Fox Paw off guard and the long blade slashed a shallow gash across Fox Paw's belly.

He pretended not to notice it, charged himself and drew blood from White Eagle's shoulder but the wound was minor. White Eagle was not in a position to counterattack.

Fox Paw bent low, grabbed a handful of dirt and threw it at White Eagle's face and at the same time drove in slashing viciously with the eight inch blade.

White Eagle got his hand over his eyes just in time to ward off the dirt, but he couldn't recover in time to avoid the blade. It drove into White Eagle's left forearm, scraping the bone. The searing pain jolted through his system making him gasp.

His own knife answered, slashing hard across

Fox Paw's right forearm, bringing a wince and a howl of pain.

At once Fox Paw shifted the blade to his left hand. During the movement White Eagle saw his chance and kicked upward hard with his right foot. The top of his foot caught Fox Paw's left wrist, snapped the bones and spun the big knife into the dirt.

White Eagle drove forward, slammed his body against the weaponless Fox Paw, throwing him to the ground on his back. White Eagle sat on the other warrior's belly and poised the big knife over Fox Paw's throat.

Both men were panting from the struggle.

"Kill me!" Fox Paw shouted. "Kill me now!"

White Eagle shook his head. "I will not. The blade is there, use your right hand and drive it into your throat if you wish. I would rather have you as a member of my band."

Fox Paw's right hand grabbed the hilt of the knife. He looked at White Eagle. His eyes went wide and bulged for a moment, then looked down at the knife. He screamed, but his hand did not move. Tears leaped to his eyes and he turned his head.

White Eagle stood, took the rawhide and slashed it in half.

The argument was over.

The fight was over.

It was forgotten.

By cutting the *muerto* rawhide strip, White Eagle had given Fox Paw permission to remain in the Eagle band.

His wife hurried up and stopped the blood from his belly and arm, then pulled his left hand forward. Fox Paw yelled in pain as she felt the broken wrist bones, meshing them together. Then she put a pair of white buffalo ribs on both sides of his wrist and bound them firmly in place with thin strips of wet rawhide. When the rawhide dried, it would tighten and hold the wrist firmly in place between the bone splints until the bones mended.

The next day when the band got ready to leave, Fox Paw and his wife and two small daughters turned away to the south. They would search out another band and join them.

White Eagle watched them go with sadness. His band needed every fighting man it could get. He wished the warrior well and reminded him of his great victories in war and raiding. Fox Paw nodded, the pain still great in his arm. But the praise from White Eagle made him sit taller on his war pony as he and his small herd of horses angled south toward the Colorado.

9

The trip north toward Mulberry Creek took the Eagle Band nearly three weeks. The third day out on a leisurely trek with the whole band, they came upon a large herd of buffalo. Since there was water nearby and plenty of graze, they made a quick hunting camp and launched one of the three or four fall hunts they would need to provide enough pemmican for the winter.

Again and again the Comanche broad-tipped buffalo arrows brought down the shaggy beasts. The women ran up and the butchering process began.

The Comanche used almost every part of the shaggy beast, from the hide to the hair, to sinews, to brains to the hooves. Each part had a dedicated plan in the Comanche way of life. Without the buffalo the Comanche nation would die quickly.

For a week, the buffalo strips hung in the hot sun. When they were dried, they were stored by each family in large rawhide boxes and tended and protected. The jerky would soon be pounded into a powder and mixed with buffalo fat and some kind of flavoring such as blueberry, blackberry, persimmon or even pecan or walnut to make pemmican. Then it would be stored for the winter needs.

Pemmican was the winter staple. With enough the band could winter over without pain. Without enough pemmican it would be known as the winter the babies cried—just before they began starving to death.

A week after the hunt began, the Eagle band moved on north toward the Peace and the tributaries of the mighty Red River. Three days later they stopped again in a sheltered grove and launched a second major hunt. The buffalo had not moved far and feared nothing, right up to the moment a Comanche arrow pierced their hearts, and they stumbled, then tumbled to the Texas high plains in a rolling jumble of fur and dust.

Then sharp knives slashed, the giant creatures, some weighing as much as a thousand pounds, were skinned out on one side, the flesh was cut from the bones and sent to the drying racks. When one half of the creature had been cut up, a pony was used to turn the carcass over so the rest of the skin could be carefully removed and the meat taken off.

Bones were saved to be formed into tools. The brains would be used later in the tanning process. Stomach liners became bags to hold small items, and water bottles. Nothing went to waste.

Through the three weeks that Doris had been a captive of White Eagle she had been treated well. She knew she was not a slave, but neither was she wife to White Eagle. Already there were three women in his tipi, but it was not crowded.

At night, when no one could hear, she sobbed for her dead husband and her small daughter, and the lives of the twenty-eight others who had lived in the small cluster of buildings. They thought that five cabins together would be safe from Comanche raids. They had been wrong, dead wrong.

Her days were filled learning what the other women did, trying to help them. She always had been good at making herself useful, and she adapted quickly to the Indian ways. The food made her ill for the first week, but soon she learned to tolerate it and eat it as a matter of course.

Most of her time was taken up caring for Daniel. The small white boy had been Bill and Barbara's son. Now he was orphaned. White Eagle delighted in the boy. When the flap was down on their tipi, he played with the small bundle for hours. Quickly White Eagle taught him to fight and wrestle, and he named the white boy, Charging Bear, because he pretended to be so ferocious when he played with the giant Indian. He was not afraid.

It had been the second week of Doris' captivity that White Eagle came to her bed. He sat on the edge of it and talked softly to her. She understand none of it, except for an English word now and then.

At last he lay beside her, and she knew what he had been trying to tell her. She had always enjoyed making love with her husband, even though she had the idea nice ladies weren't supposed to. Now she discovered new and tantalizing lovemaking with this tall Indian.

She tried to figure it out. Nothing was that

much different, but perhaps it was just the thought of being caressed and then entered by a *savage* that set her on fire. She responded with such fire and desire that their lovemaking often turned into noisy, laughing, yelling affairs that surprised the other women in the tipi.

For ten nights in a row, White Eagle planted his seed deep within her. He had made her understand the second night that he wanted her to get pregnant.

Doris knew she was not pregnant by her husband when she was captured. After the first shock wore off, she realized that she *wanted to get pregnant* by this tall, darkly handsome Comanche, even though she knew she couldn't. She knew she was being disloyal to her dead husband and all of her friends, but this was reality, here and now. She had to live and this was the way right now to make sure of it. White Eagle would not sell her to another band, or let anyone harm her if he thought she were pregnant with his child!

When White Eagle left her that night, she found Daniel and checked him where he slept in the softest buffalo robe. He was a tough little one. He had adapted much already and was learning Comanche words. If he stayed there for two years, he would be a Comanche forever!

Doris had made friends at once with Laughing Golden Hair. They talked English with each other, and both helped White Eagle learn more English words. Laughing Golden Hair was so pretty that Doris wondered about her own looks. Her hair was still braided. She hadn't washed it since she was captured. She'd do that tomorrow.

Later that same day, Laughing Golden Hair

caught Doris's hand and pulled her toward the
creek. She wanted to show her a new patch of
berries she had found.

White Eagle watched them go. His face showed
no emotion. But he was pleased. His last two
captives were working out well. Soon the tall
white Doris would be pregnant and growing a son
for him. Then he would have two sons!

Already he had started teaching Charging Bear
how to shoot the small bow and arrow he had
made for him. The boy was quick to learn. He
would make a fine chief.

White Eagle took out the soft leather pouch
with a drawstring of rawhide lacing and fingered
the *tosi-tivo* gold. It was called gold money, and
Doris had told him it was greatly valuable.

He remembered the trader who had come in a
broken wagon with goods for sale. The wandering
half white man knew no Comanche tongue, but
drove a hard bargain.

At first White Eagle had bargained with
horses. The trader had four rifles, and White
Eagle wanted them. Instead of twenty horses for
each rifle, White Eagle offered the trader one of
the gold coins for each rifle.

The trader had been so surprised to see the gold
he couldn't cover up his eagerness. He demanded
three coins for each rifle, but at last took one. For
one more of the coins, the trader sold the
Comanche the rest of his stock of beads and
trinkets and ends of cloth. The Comanche women
were delighted.

Now White Eagle stared at the sack of gold
coins. He had counted them. There were more
than fifty. How had one small rancher found so
much of the woman's clay? White Eagle shook

his head in amazement, then put the gold away where it was safe from prying eyes. No one except Doris knew that he had the gold coins. Some day he would need them.

Sadie was happier than she had been in weeks. Having another "mother" in the tipi was a joy, especially since she could speak English. Sadie had cried when she told Doris about the raid by the Indians on the supply train and how so many had died.

She wasn't sure what happened to her mother and brother.

"When will my father come to get us?" Sadie asked.

Doris held her tightly. There was no way she could tell the small child that her father had come with the Pony Soldiers when they were at the Croton Creek camp. Her father and his soldiers had not been able to defeat the Comanche.

Now they were going north again, away from the Pony Soldiers. Doris felt hot tears creep down her cheeks. She realized that this was not just a vacation, or a pleasant outing. She suddenly understood that she could be here with the Comanche for the rest of her life!

At once she hardened her mind, she would accept the kindness and the loving of the Comanche, but she would from this day forward wait and watch, and look for a way to escape. When she found it she would take Daniel and Sadie and they would slip away and find their way to the nearest settlement. It would have to be a good plan. Just walking away would not work. Even with good fast ponies the Comanche would catch them quickly.

It had to be an excellent plan, and it had to be

the next time the Pony Soldiers found them. Yes, that was it. She had to plan and watch and wait. When the Pony Soldiers came she would escape with her two small charges!

Sadie had wondered about all the talk about the Pony Soldiers after the raid, but she did not connect it with her father. If her father had been that close he would have come and taken her away to the fort. She was sure of that. So it must have been some other Pony Soldiers who didn't know she was there.

She had found a bow one of the older boys had outgrown, and she was learning to shoot arrows. It was a lot harder than she thought. One of her tipi sisters helped her. Black Bird was more than seven years old and could use a bow and arrow well. She was White Eagle's daughter and patiently showed Laughing Golden Hair how to shoot with the bow. She helped her again and again, and after a while, the white girl got the idea. Then it was a matter of practice. She would learn to shoot a bow as well as Black Bird and Something Pretty, her other tipi sister who was also five.

The three girls ran to the stream but it was too cold to go swimming. They splashed a minute, then sat on the bank letting the growing colder sun warm them.

For an hour they took out the curved buffalo bones the older women used for sticks to hit the buffalo hair-stuffed ball. They knocked it up and down a grassy field until they were all exhausted. A cold drink from the stream and a handful of berries refreshed them, and they walked back to the big tipi arm in arm.

Laughing Golden Hair had tanned well these

last three months. She was almost the same copper color as her tipi sisters. All of the small rope burns had healed and each day it seemed her hair grew longer. Cries In The Morning loved to grease and then braid it in proper Indian fashion.

Some days Sadie thought about home a lot. On those days she ran to find Doris and they talked about their homes and what the other white people were doing. They always went off by themselves to say these things, so no one would hear them.

Today, Sadie wandered around the tipis watching people. She was about to check in one of the other tipis for a friend when an Indian boy ran between the tipis shouting and waving his bow and arrows at everyone he saw.

White Eagle stepped from his tipi and scowled at the boy for a minute, then he pulled his lance from where it stood beside his buffalo shield in front of his tipi and ran to where the boy stood threatening one of the old men.

White Eagle stopped eight feet from the youth.

"Lame Beaver, put down your bow. We are your friends here. This is your band."

Lame Beaver turned toward White Eagle. His eyes were wide and wild. There was a strange expression on his face, and as he breathed through his mouth, flecks of foam came out.

The youth yelled. It was not a Comanche war cry. They were not words, but a terrible cry of an animal who had been wounded. As he screamed, Lame Beaver notched an arrow and lifted the bow with the arrow aimed at the band's leader.

White Eagle swung his lance—the butt end of it jolted into Lame Beaver's bow before he could draw, slammed it out of his hands and then the lance thrust again. The second time it struck Lame Beaver in the back, over his kidney just above his hip bone and he sank slowly to his knees, then fell to one side, the screams still spilling from his mouth.

Quickly White Eagle ran to the boy, turned him on his back and tied his hands behind him with a piece of rawhide thong. Now Lame Beaver was spitting the white bubbles from his mouth. He tried to talk, but couldn't. His eyes were like a caged animal's now.

His screams came again and again.

Three women ran up, but White Eagle motioned them back. Lame Beaver's mother came rushing through the group but she stopped when she saw him. He lay on his side, his legs drawn up to his chest, his face a froth of foam.

His mother took a step back and looked at White Eagle.

"Yes, you're right. Somehow Lame Beaver has caught the Foaming Dog Mouth. Every dog in camp must be tied up so it can touch no one and no other dog or animal. We must do it now or more of us will be struck down by this disease."

Doris came around a tipi, caught Laughing Golden Hair's hand and led her away from the place.

"We don't want to see any more of that," Doris said. She knelt in front of Sadie. "Do you know what he has?"

Sadie shook her head.

"It's called a lot of things, but our people used the word rabies. Just terrible. It can get in a pack of wolves and bats and cats and dogs and kill just everything. If a rabid dog bites a man he can get it, too. He always—" She stopped. "Let's go back to the tipi and see if they find what bit the boy."

Doris kept Sadie inside the tipi the rest of the afternoon.

White Eagle had talked with the council. Lame Beaver had been on his vision quest, he had been on two raids. He was almost a warrior. But it had to be done.

Two warriors had been watching Lame Beaver, not letting him move from where he had fallen. Two other warriors had gone to Lame Beaver's mother's tipi and looked for his dog. Lame Beaver had two dogs he was proud of. They went everywhere with him, hunted with him. Only one was at the tipi.

They reported that Lame Beaver's one dog was tied inside the tipi. Every warrior in camp now searched the area for Lame Beaver's second dog. It took them an hour to find it. The dog had dug a hole and crawled under the back of a tipi, burrowing almost out of sight.

It snarled and snapped at them, foam flickering around its mouth. The warrior who found the dog called White Eagle. He took a club and coaxed the snarling animal half out of the hole, then smashed its skull with one blow from the heavy club.

"Do not touch it!" White Eagle bellowed. He found a strong stick and cut a sharp point on the end. With the point he stabbed into the dog's carcass and carried it far up on the hill. He had brought a spade taken on a raid. Quickly the dog's body was buried deep in the ground and covered.

Back at the camp, the council had decided another important step. Three of the women were told to build a lean-to shelter a hundred yards up the hill. They were to make it rainproof and windproof. A pole of dead wood was found. They cut it off three feet long and made a point on the end.

When the lean-to was completed of brush and boughs from the pecan trees and the live oaks, White Eagle went to Lame Beaver. He did not try to talk to him. Lame Beaver's soul was not willing to talk with anyone.

White Eagle lifted him by the arms, and staying behind him, walked Lame Beaver up the hill. At the shelter the heavy stake was pounded into the ground using a large rock. When it remained only a foot out of the soil, a dozen stout pieces of rawhide were tied to the stake, then Lame Beaver was tied to the stake by his ankles, and by his wrists.

His hands were moved in front of him. When White Eagle was sure that Lame Beaver could not get away, the warriors left him. One warrior stood twenty yards away. Someone would guard him day and night.

All the rest of the day, Lame Beaver screamed and howled and cried. Those in the camp below tried not to listen. Every dog in camp was eyed with suspicion. They would stay tied up for fifteen days, then if none showed signs of the foaming dog mouth disease, the camp could get back to normal.

The second day, Lame Beaver stopped screaming. He had yelled so much that his voice would no longer function. No one went near him. The Comanche had seen rabies before. They had found it in bats and wolves and coyotes and rabbits.

Only once before could White Eagle remember one of the People having it. The warrior had killed three women and a child before he had been killed. The sickness had turned him into a raging animal.

"Crazy Mouth" some of the People called it. Hopefully they had stopped it before anyone else had caught the disease. White Eagle was not sure how Lame Beaver caught it, but it usually came from a dog. Now they would watch and hope.

Lame Beaver went into convulsions the third day. His body shook and jolted and he wailed in misery. No one was allowed to approach his lean-to.

The fourth day Lame Beaver died. When no sound came from the lean-to for three hours, White Eagle went up to the hill. The boy was dead. The sickness had died with him. White Eagle made his family leave him there for two more days, then his body was carried in a buffalo robe to the highest peak within a days ride and given the traditional burial, so his spirit could lift into the clouds.

White Eagle made them leave the robe there with the body. They came back wailing and crying. His mother slashed her arms to show her grief, and let blood spread down the horse she rode. Only when she was back at the camp did she close up her wounds.

White Eagle visited every tipi the next day. Nowhere did he find anyone sick. None of the dogs were showing any signs of the rabies. They had stopped Lame Beaver in time. He went back to his tipi and played with little Charging Bear. In two or three days they would have to go to a hunting camp. It was time. The leaves were falling. Winter was coming. Two more hunting times and they would be ready for their winter camp.

Then White Eagle would have endless days to play with Charging Bear, teach him to become a chief, and to watch Doris's belly swell with the growth of his own son. She must have a son!

10

Red Hawk had watched Lame Beaver die. They had been good friends. Red Hawk did not understand why his friend was gone, why he would never seen him again. The gods struck down a promising young warrior for no reason. It only made him all the more ready to go and confront the gods. He was ready now. Perhaps that was part of Lame Beaver's reason for dying—to help show Red Hawk his path in life.

Red Hawk sat in front of his father's tipi for an hour after Lame Beaver died. Then he went to two of the Old Men and talked to them about a vision quest. Each told him something different. Each gave him some idea of what he should do and how to do it. Then he went and sat outside White Eagle's tipi waiting until he was asked to speak.

White Eagle came back from the lean-to on the side of the hill, he saw Red Hawk but did not acknowledge him. He went into his tipi and a half hour later came out and motioned Red Hawk to follow him. They went to the council fire logs where White Eagle sat and indicated that Red Hawk should stand and speak.

"Great Chief White Eagle, I am ready to begin my vision quest. I have spoken with the Old Men, learning from them what I can. Now I wish your instruction, advice and counsel."

White Eagle had done this service many times before for young men as they went on their vision quests. It was a time when each new warrior-to-be must purify himself, prostrate himself to the gods, and ask their direction. Each one hoped for a vision to lead him on his journey through life. At the same time he might learn his new name through some natural happening during his quest.

"Red Hawk, you have prepared yourself for this quest. You know the rituals of obedience to the gods. You know you must be pure in spirit to have a vision, and your quest for that vision is one of the most important acts of your life."

"Yes, White Eagle. I understand all of this."

"You know that you may take enough jerky or pemmican for only two days. If your quest lasts longer you must live off the strength of your body and your spirit."

"I understand all of this."

"Who created Mother Earth upon which we all live?"

"The council of the gods made the land and all that is in and on it. The gods of the council are the gods of the wind, of the thunder, of rain, of the trees and of the buffalo and horses. The gods all join together, and I seek their guidance through a vision of my destiny in life, of my work, of my duties as a Comanche warrior!"

"Then begin your quest. Take only your knife,

breechclout and moccasins. Treat every rock, every tree, every hill and valley as one of the gods of the People. May you be successful, Red Hawk, in your vision quest!''

White Eagle stood and stared at the youth for a moment, then Red Hawk spun on his foot and walked slowly out of camp toward the north and the highest mountain he could see. He wanted to find his vision high in the sky overlooking as much of Mother Earth as possible.

Red Hawk did not run, nor jog. He knew he had to conserve his energies for the ritual ordeal that was to come. He did not understand all of it. Other boys who had been on their vision quest had told him parts of it. He knew he must find a favorite place and plead with the gods to grant him a vision. Then he must sit and meditate until it happened.

It might take a day, it might take a week or even two weeks. He would have to know how long he could wait and pray for the quest, before he had to leave to get back to the camp.

Once in a great while a young man came back without receiving a vision. He was allowed one more chance. Failing that, he would have to go through life never becoming a warrior, never able to take a wife. He would do menial jobs for the band for the rest of his life.

Red Hawk walked until it grew dark. He was about half way to the peak he had selected. It was not much of a mountain, but it was the best he could find in this part of the high Texas plains.

He had heard the less water you drank, the quicker you would have the vision. He drank sparingly as he went across small streams, then not at all as he climbed up the low hills in front of the higher ridge.

When night came he sat against a rock and watched the stars. There were dozens of star gods, but he couldn't remember their names. Names weren't as important as listening for them to speak to you. Red Hawk sat very still listening, watching the scudding clouds block out the moon and the stars.

But none of them spoke to him.

He ate a little of the jerky, chewing it for as long as he could before he had to swallow it. Sometime before the Big Dipper fell from the sky, he slept.

Morning came and the warm glow of the fall sun shone on him. He had not felt cold. Often he felt cold even under his buffalo robes in his parent's tipi.

Good! It was the first sign that he would have a successful vision quest!

He hiked up the hill again, went over one ridge, then another and about noon came to the top of the ridge. He could see for many days walk in each direction. He had brought along some of the sacred powder from the Medicine Man and now pinched it with his thumb and finger and tossed a pinch in each of the four directions, imploring the gods to see and hear him, and to grant him a vision and a serious task for his life.

After he scattered the sacred powder, he sat down on a large slab of rock, crossed his legs, and put his hands on his thighs. He sat that way for two hours, but no one spoke to him. Nothing happened.

Once a curious Eagle circled high overhead, dove to within twenty feet of him, then retreated with a call of rage because his hoped-for prey turned out to be his greatest enemy, man.

For the next two days Red Hawk sat on the slab of rock. He was warm in the day and cold at night. He slept sometimes, but tried to stay awake. He had eaten nothing the last two days, hoping to save his meager food for the walk home.

The third day he had trouble sitting up. A film seemed to come down over his eyes and he blinked to get rid of it. He began to sing his song of life, making it up as he went along. The wonders of his life, the glories of the People, the marvels of the Eagle Band. But he didn't feel inspired, the songs came out dull and routine.

He put sharp stones between his toes so the pain would keep him alert. His stomach began to hurt and then he vomited. He was dizzy most of the afternoon. At last he moved to a stone with sharp edges, and put small rocks to sit on to help him keep awake.

He wanted to sleep.

He feared if he slept he would never awake.

The dizziness came again and he fell to the rocks, gashing his forehead. Blood ran down his face.

He had not noticed the storm clouds rushing toward him. Lightning snarled from the clouds to the ground. Lightning was a sign of the gods' anger. Then to reinforce the anger came the roaring thunder as the gods banged the earth against the clouds to show their continuing unhappiness.

Rain drenched Red Hawk. It revived him. He sat up straight again on the sharp rocks. He put a round pebble in his mouth and sucked on it. For a moment his stomach felt better.

With the rain came a cold wind, and flakes of

snow dropped, then they were replaced with hail the size of pheasant eggs. The hailstones were not hard, but soft and broke when they hit him.

He laughed at them. He could crush hail stones! The hail stones hit his face and came away red with his blood. He laughed again and welcomed the gods' testing him.

Then the dizziness came back and he fell forward, protecting himself with his hands and lay there as the rain and hail pounded down on him.

From far off he saw a large black stallion racing toward him. The stallion had eyes of green anger, and smoke and flames blazed from his nostrils. Steam issued from the great horse's mouth as he raced up the mountain and stood panting and heaving at Red Hawk's side.

"Get on my back," the horse said to him.

Red Hawk was not surprised to hear the horse speak. At once he jumped up and leaped on the bare back of the black stallion and they raced away, only they were no longer on the ground. They sailed in the air. Below he saw the Eagle Band camp on Mulberry Creek. He watched as they flew over the rolling plains and into the desert and the sparse growth and over the high snow covered mountains he had heard about that were two moons journey to the west.

These mountains always had snow, even in the hottest summer, and they were covered with huge forests of trees so tall it would take all day to walk around one that had fallen to the ground.

Red Hawk saw men and machines he didn't understand. He saw long strings of wagons with white covers on them, and white eyes plodding along beside the wagons or driving cattle along behind them.

He saw a huge steam belching horse made of iron that was ten horses long, and clattered along on shining ribbons of metal that extended so far into the distance that they at last came together into a single point.

He found a company of Pony Soldiers ride against him and his black stallion, and he was a mighty warrior and crushed the whole company, killing each one and racing back to show White Eagle the forty rifles and forty pistols that he alone had captured. His scalp pole was bending so it broke when he hung all forty scalps on it.

He kept asking the black horse what it meant, but the stallion pretended that he couldn't talk, merely flew around and let Red Hawk see all the parts of his vision.

Then slowly the big horse settled back down on the same ledge they had left from. As Red Hawk dismounted he asked the stallion again what it all meant.

The stallion snorted and pawed the ground with his front hooves. "I only bring you to the vision, I am not allowed to tell you what it means. That is up to you to figure out."

Then, as Red Hawk began to ask him another question, the black stallion vanished in a wisp of mist. The mist too was gone and Red Hawk slumped to the ground and fainted.

When he woke, the warm sun was up high. The ground looked as if the snow and rain had never come.

He had his vision!

Red Hawk remembered it all perfectly. He would determine its meaning as he went back down the mountain. He found the rest of his food in the small rawhide bag he brought with him and ate. Then he was strong enough to start down.

He had discovered no new name signs. Nothing had approached him. He would keep his name since none other was ordered. He would be Red Hawk, and soon a warrior!

As he walked down the slope he began to evaluate his quest and to translate each of the symbolic events into day-by-day duties he must undertake for the tribe. He was far from finished by the time he hiked back to the camp on Mulberry Creek the second day.

His heart stopped a moment when he saw the bare banks of the creek. Only a few indications were left that a band had camped there. At once he knew what he had to do. He searched the woods near where the horses were kept. After half an hour he found his pony with a long tether in fresh grass.

All he had to do was look for the tracks of the band and follow them to the hunting camp they would establish. Again they had headed north and some to the west.

The caprock could almost be seen from here. Perhaps some day they would go all the way to the Staked Plains!

Red Hawk mounted the pony and rode to the far end of the camp where he saw the most tracks. Soon he had found the travois pole marks in the dust. He rode out at a natural canter. He would find the band within a day or two at the most.

Red Hawk smiled. He had found his vision, he would soon be a warrior! It was a good day to be alive!

11

After the standoff with White Eagle at Croton Creek, Captain Colt Harding pushed his men hard. They arrived back at Fort Comfort after a little over two days riding.

The men were frustrated that they had not had a chance to close with the Comanche in battle. The Tonkawas were furious that they were not given the one Comanche killed so they could enjoy some of their special "soup."

Most bothered of all was Captain Harding. He had a strong feeling that his daughter was so close that day that he could have almost touched her, yet she was a continent away. White Eagle possessed one bargaining chip in this poker game that Captain Harding could not top.

If the army kept pressuring him to release Sadie, or of the Pony Soldiers moved in too close, White Eagle could kill his captive. The savages held that advantage that the white men would never have.

So Captain Harding had to develop a whole new plan to rescue Sadie. He would still use his

Lightning Company as an example of how the army should be fighting the hostiles. He had received one favorable letter about the plan from Colonel Sparkman in San Antonio, headquarters of the Division of Texas.

But for Sadie it would have to be something else. Perhaps a surprise raid by him and the Tonkawas. Another leave of absence. Move so the Comanche scouts never knew they were within a hundred miles. Creep into their camp at night, grab Sadie from the big tipi and be gone in the darkness before the Comanche knew anything had happened.

He had threatened to do it that way before, but it involved tremendous risks. His whole career, his very life was in the worst kind of jeopardy. The Tonks might even decide to use him for their stews and steaks and barbequed ribs! They could say the Comanche had killed him.

At the fort the returning company was met by a six man escort. The three wounded were moved in first, then the rest came in as smartly as they could.

In his quarters, Captain Harding looked over the dispatches which Lt. Riddle had sorted through. There had been only one come in.

Lt. Riddle watched his commander. He poured them each a shot glass of whiskey and handed one to the Captain.

"You contacted White Eagle?"

Captain Harding lifted the shot glass and drank it down in one blast. He coughed and put the glass on the desk.

"Hell yes. The Breed talked to him like a cousin. The only problem was White Eagle threatened Sadie if we didn't vamoose. He had us blackjacked. We left."

"Damn." Lt. Riddle pointed to the dispatches. "Nothing important in there. Routine. We're getting in some more rifle rounds, and twenty new Spencer repeaters. Maybe someday every man will have the same make and caliber of weapon."

Lt. Riddle walked to the window and came back. His face was strained, he seemed uncomfortable. Harding noticed it at once.

"All right, John. Tell me what the hell went wrong. You've been acting like you were heading into battle for the first time. Tell me."

"Yeah, hard man to fool. We've got a little bit of a problem. Day after you left, we had some visitors. Five covered wagons pulled up to the gate. We've got five families who want to homestead nearby. The men are out riding, looking around for the best spots. Three of them want to be cattle ranchers, as I recall, and the other two will be dirt farmers, sod busters."

"Homesteaders! Way out here? Christ! I thought the folks at Austin said nobody was to come out this far."

"Did. But Austin isn't the authority on government land. Nobody told them not to come, so here they are. They say they figured to locate nearby so the fort can protect them."

"Where are they camped? We'll go pay them a social call tomorrow."

"Downstream on the White, maybe a half mile. They settled in just above the Indian camp."

"Exactly what I need, five homestead families to worry about. They said we were supposed to protect them?"

"True. They've been here for five days now,

getting impatient to drive in some stakes.''

Captain Harding swore in a whisper for two minutes, never repeating himself. He unbuttoned his blue uniform shirt. "See if I've got a clean shirt in the bureau, we better get out there right now and send them back to Austin.''

Lt. Riddle, Captain Harding and six men from B Company rode out a half hour later. The wagons could be seen from just outside the fort at their downstream location.

As they rode up, the officers saw that the wagons had been pulled into a defensive circle. Three cooking fires were going, and twenty or thirty civilians wandered around inside and outside the wagon ring. To the left was a rope corral filled with horses, mules and a few steers. It was an unholy grouping.

A man came forward. He was one of the ranchers. Cowboy hat, boots, and a gunbelt with a new looking hogleg.

"Evening, Captain, heard you and your men just got back. Sorry to hear you didn't rescue your little girl, Sadie. Oh, I'm Josh Wilson.''

Captain Harding swung down off his horse and shook hands with Wilson.

"Pleased to meet you, Mr. Wilson. I hope you've reconsidered homesteading this far from the safety of other settlers. It's absolutely far too dangerous out here. We're a hundred and twenty miles from Austin, and two years ago some Comanches raided farms not two miles from Austin.''

"Know that, Captain. We're here. We know where it is. We're setting out stakes in the morning to claim our homesteads. Afraid that decision is made, not one you have any authority over."

"But you'll want me to risk my troopers and officers to defend you when the Comanche find out you're here. They hate four-wallers worse than anything. You'll be throwing a life and death challenge right in their teeth."

"Progress, I guess you'd call it, Captain Harding. Sorry, but we're here to stay."

Wilson was a tall, stringy man, who moved with an easy stride and had a casual relaxed appearance that probably belied his quickness and ability with his six-gun. Captain Harding had seen a man or two like him before. Gambler. Wilson had been a gambler at one time or another.

"Captain, the five of us worked it out. For the first few years we'll all live in a compound of five houses, built close together and inside a solid wall. We figure we can make the houses and the wall out of this adobe clay blocks like you made your fort of. We got our carpenter building us the form boxes now and we found a new deposit of clay. We'll be on the White River here about another mile down, where the valley spreads out and there's plenty of grass and the trees are still standing along the creeks."

"Wilson. There isn't any chance that I can let you stay here. I do have authority over undeveloped areas."

"True Captain, but once we get our stakes down, this area becomes developed. Talked to the State Attorney General in Austin, and to the army's liaison man there. He gave me a letter for you."

Captain Harding took the letter and held it. "I know what it's going to say, Mr. Wilson. But do you know what a man looks like after the Comanches scalp him and then mutilate the body?"

"That I do, Captain. Not a pretty sight."

"And have you seen a ranch or farm after a Comanche raid? You know what they do to the women and children?"

"I do, Captain. I fought with the cavalry for two years back in fifty-seven. We did a mite of Comanche work ourselves with the Second Cavalry."

"Then I shouldn't have to tell you the danger."

"You don't. We didn't come here for your permission, your approval, or for your anger. We're here, and we're going to stay here. We'll have three cattle ranches and two farms all picked out. In a year or two we should be able to provide you most of your beef, vegetables, beans, potatoes, and wheat and oats for your stock. We can save the army the cost of transport from Austin. I've already put in a bid with the District of Texas Army Headquarters Quartermaster to supply you."

"Thought of everything, haven't you, Wilson?"

"I hope so. We're risking the lives of thirty-two human beings out here. We're going to see that the plan works. For our first herds we'll gather up the strays we've been spotting. I figure there are at least fifty thousand head of cattle running wild in this part of Texas. Most of them were cut loose during the war, and just never rounded up."

"Mr. Wilson, I'll see that target practice is conducted away from your compound, and that your homestead and buildings will be off limits to my troopers and officers. You're welcome to the fort at any time."

"Well, that's mighty neighborly of you, Captain Harding and Lieutenant Riddle. Now that the formalities are over, would you like to meet the rest of our people?"

"Sorry, Mr. Wilson, I'm just back from a sixty-five mile ride and I'm wanting a bath. Perhaps at a later time." Captain Harding stepped up on his horse and Lieutenant Edwards followed. They said goodbye and cantered back to the fort.

"Two of the girls in the group are over sixteen," Lt. Riddle said. "They could present us with some problems."

"Off limits," Captain Harding growled. "Any man who touches those civilians gets twenty years pounding rocks!"

They rode a hundred yards.

"How is our eighteen-year-old trouble maker doing?"

"Pamela. She hasn't caused any more explosions that I know of. She has been causing her father some gray hairs, though I'd say. Captain Kenny will be leaving tomorrow morning on a three day sweep patrol. He requested a second one to get a feel of the country."

"Good. He's going to be a fine addition to our staff."

Back at Captain Harding's quarters, Cpl. Swenson had two boilers of hot water waiting on the stove. Colt Harding tried to soak away some of his anger and his mounting problems.

Farther down the officer country side of Fort Comfort, Captain Morse Kenny stood in front of his daughter, Pamela. Both were angry. Both had already said things that they shouldn't have, but a stubborn streak common to both refused to let them recant.

Pamela set her fists on her hips and glared at her father. "Yes! I said I love him. I want to marry him. I don't care if he's *only a corporal* as you said. A man is a man, and he's as good as any officer on this post!"

"He hasn't even been to school past the fourth grade. He doesn't know who his father was." Captain Kenny threw up his hands and sat down in his chair. "I don't understand you, Pamela."

"Obviously, Father. I'm not a little girl. I'm a woman. I have the desires and needs of a woman. That's why we get married. I will marry Victor whether you want me to or not. And just to make certain, I'm warning you. If you try to interfere, I'll go straight to Captain Harding and tell him how you beat up on Victor when he hadn't done a damn thing!"

Kenny jumped up. "Stop swearing, Pamela. And I'm sure you wouldn't tell Captain Harding!"

"I would, I will! Now just settle down and get used to the idea of having a grandchild. I want maybe six kids."

"You couldn't turn in your own father?"

"If you try to stop Vic and me, I most certainly will. His enlistment is up in two months. We'll go to Austin and be married there. Write to auntie and tell her I won't be coming to Boston."

"This is insane!"

Captain Kenny still thought the whole idea of his long protected daughter falling into the clutches of a lowly corporal was disgusting. He led his patrol out the next morning, and for the first time he had included Cpl. Victor Gregory in the roster. He could at least see how the man functioned in the field.

Even so, the idea of an enlisted man for a son-in-law was ridiculous, totally unacceptable. It would be awkward even having them over for supper some night. No other officers could be present, that would be for certain.

He sighed, led the twenty man patrol out the gate and sighted in on his compass, then headed into the sector he needed to sweep to be sure there was no Comanche activity. It was about twenty miles west of the fort. They would be on the site before midday.

The patrol moved along well toward the objective, a small hill called Rooster's Knob. They covered the twenty miles and took a break. At this point the usual procedure was to split the patrol in half. One unit would sweep around the west side of the knob and down a long valley often used by Comanches.

The second element would take the eastern side, move up a different low valley and they would meet some ten miles north.

Captain Kenny had never liked the idea of splitting up a force of any size when there were hostiles around. But it was the only way to cover the ground they had to in three days. He sent Sgt. Dean Franklin with the first squad and he took the second. He made sure that Cpl. Gregory remained with him. He wanted to keep an eye on the young man.

Captain Kenny talked with his sergeant.

"Do the sweep and stay out of trouble," Kenny cautioned. "I don't like splitting up. Don't start a fight with any Comanche you see. They'll probably run if they see you first. We'll meet at the head of the two valleys sometime around two hours from now."

151

"Yes, sir. Should be no problem. We've all done this before."

"Except me, Sergeant. I'll try to measure up. Move out."

Captain Kenny had felt his face flush at the unintentional slap in the face Sergeant Franklin gave him. He was the new kid on the block even if he was a captain. Another few months and he'd have his garrison duty tag shaken off.

He moved out his men at a ground-eating canter. It was the roughest way for a man to sit a horse, but it was a natural pace for most horses, and they could maintain it for hours without tiring.

For this operation they were in a two abreast formation, with Captain Kenny at the head of the small column. He watched behind them and saw that they were sending up a thin cloud of dust. If there were Comanche in the area, they would know someone was coming.

The patrol flushed through the dry course of a small stream. It probably had run during the spring and halfway into summer. It had watered a half dozen pecan trees and a few live oak. They rode through the trees and brush, found no evidence of an Indian camp and moved on up the flat, dry valley.

A hawk circled high over the landscape. They saw no game. To the far left Captain Kenny thought he saw a moving brown mass which could be a herd of slowly grazing buffalo. He had never actually seen buffalo up close. He was anxious to put that small problem behind him.

Cpl. Gregory rode up beside him.

"Sir. To the left ahead there's a dust trail. About two fingers off north, sir."

Kenny looked in that direction and saw the trail. It was a much larger trail than their own, which meant more horses. He held up his hand and the patrol stopped.

"If it's a raiding party, they'll want to check us out and see if we're a wagon train or settlers," Gregory said.

Captain Kenny remembered that Gregory had won his stripes in the field before he went to the clerk's job.

"Corporal, how many riders would you guess are out there?"

Gregory looked at them again, then at the sun. He paused. "Hate to say it, sir, but I'd figure twenty, or twenty-five. They're turned and are coming directly at us."

"Not shy, are they?"

"Not the Comanche, sir, in what he considers his own front yard."

They were a mile from the closest cover of any kind. Even the pecan trees had deserted them.

"That grove about a mile to the left," Capt. Kenny said quickly. "We'll head for that and see if they want to fight."

'Ho-oooooooooo," Captain Kenny called and swung his arm forward. The patrol galloped half way to the trees, then cantered the rest of the way. The dust of the riders came closer. By the time they were in the cover of the trees, the hostiles could be seen. They were Comanche.

"At least twenty-five," Kenny said. "Move the horses back, tie them and get the wrangler back up here," Kenny barked at Cpl. Gregory.

Five minutes later the men of the first squad of B Company lay behind downed logs and hastily pulled up rock barricades as a Comanche raiding party held a small council just out of the best rifle range.

They ended the pow-wow and fanned out in a long line, then the center of it broke for the trees, charging in the form of a wide "V" of Comanche warriors.

"Hold your fire until I give the command to fire!" Kenny shouted. The men held. At three hundred yards they looked at the new captain. At two hundred yards they began to sweat.

When the Indians reached a hundred yards the Comanches began firing rifles.

"Fire!" Captain Kenny shouted.

The officer aimed his new Spencer and squeezed off a round. One of the lead ponies took his round in its head and stumbled and fell. One down.

The ragged volley that came from the brush killed two of the frontal charging Comanches, and put down three horses. The raiders never came within more than fifty yards of the cavalrymen.

They wheeled and raced back to a safer range.

"They'll be back, Captain," Cpl. Gregory said.

"Casualties?" Kenny bellowed. Only one man was hit. He had a crease along one shoulder.

"The next time they come, shoot for their ponies. Head shots on the horses. Without their war ponies they are helpless. You hear me? No sentimental slobs here. Gun down their mounts and we'll save our scalps."

The men acknowledged his command.

For a moment, Captain Kenny thought of sending someone to bring back the rest of their patrol. With another ten guns here the Comanche would turn tail and ride off.

Gregory. He could send the corporal on the mission and he might be spotted by the

Comanche and captured. For just a fraction of a second Captain Kenny realized that would be a good way to get rid of a major problem with Pamela.

He rejected it out of hand. Cpl. Gregory was the highest non-com he had in his group.

"Be coming back soon, sir. This time I'd guess they'll put half their men behind us. Usual Indians ain't too good at tactics, but this bunch seems to be following orders pretty damn good."

"Suggestions, Corporal Gregory?"

"Yeah, but it better wait a minute. We got visitors again."

This time the Comanche attacked in a long line riding past the clot of gunmen in the pecans and live oaks. They hung on the off side of their mounts offering no target to the cavalrymen. The squad followed its orders and fired at the horses. Two went down dead, two more were wounded and turned out of the line limping back out of range.

"Next time they'll split up, try to get two or three savages into the brush," Cpl. Gregory said. "Can't let them penetrate or we'll be in trouble."

Captain Kenny filled one of the magazine tubes with .52 caliber rounds and watched Gregory.

"You said you might have a suggestion, Corporal."

"Yes sir. This bunch ain't gonna go away. They took dead and they'll want to take our scalps. I'd say it's a raiding party heading toward Austin. We better get Sgt. Franklin and his men. Wind's blowing away from him, so chances are he won't hear the gunfire. There's a cut across country this side of the knob. I could catch him and get him back here in about an hour."

"Risky. Won't the Comanche chase you?"

"Not if you give me that big gray you're riding. It can outdistance anything they've got."

"You could get killed, Gregory."

"Yes, sir. But the odds are better if we get some help. We didn't bring that much extra ammo."

"Go, Gregory. Now, before they attack again. Get out of the back side of the brush and you can be a half mile away before they see you. Good luck."

Gregory gave him a half smile, filled another empty magazine tube and put it through the stock of his Spencer. Then he saluted and crawled back toward the horses.

Captain Kenny watched him go, then looked out front again. "Casualties?" he called.

"Yeah, Captain. Ingles down here is hit bad. Took a round in one lung I'd guess. He's out of it for now, leastwise."

"We've got help coming, Franklin. So we just hold out. If you can't get an Indian target, kill his god damned pony. They won't fight without their horses. They value those war ponies much more than they do their wives. So shoot for the horses!"

"Here they come again," someone said.

They rode past in a line again, hanging off the far side of their horses. By this time there were only four rifles firing from the Indian ranks. Captain Kenny listened for the shots from the riders and tried to hit the horses where he thought the rifle shot came from.

The charge was closer, and half of the braves used bows and arrows now. They moved in closer yet.

Another Indian pony went down. Captain

Kenny waited for the rider to kick free. As soon as the warrior stood up he hesitated. Kenny fired and the brave went down with a .52 caliber slug through his heart.

The Indians turned at the far end and came back, hanging on the other side of their mount this time.

"God help us!" Captain Kenny breathed and aimed at another Indian pony.

12

Cpl. Victor Gregory slid through the brush and
trees to the back of the small fringe of woods
along the small creek, caught the big sturdy gray
the captain rode and mounted.

If he galloped due north out of the brush the
trees would screen him from the Comanche out
front for a while. Then it would be up to the horse
and a flat out gallop for as long as he could take
it.

Gregory thought of nothing else but the troops
as he cantered north until he looked back and
could see the Indians in another attack. He
kicked the big gray into a gallop. He responded at
once, pounding north and now to the west toward
the other valley past the knob of a peak.

As he watched behind he could see no pursuit.
But even with the Comanches that could be
misleading. They might have sent two men
charging along gullies and behind ribbons of
brush just out of sight.

He rode hard for a half mile, then eased off and
let the gray blow as he walked him. Then he

galloped again. He had been right, the gray was powerful and strong. Again after another walk Gregory pushed the big horse across a wide flat area. At the far side he looked back.

If the Comanche had sent anyone after him, they had to cross this treeless flat. No one showed up. He would need another half hour, perhaps more to find Sgt. Franklin. He hoped the sergeant stopped at the small water hole about halfway to the meeting spot.

Back at the fringe of trees that protected the first squad, Captain Kenny cautioned his men.

"Let's start conserving our ammunition. Don't fire unless you have a good target, either a Comanche or a horse. I mean a head shot on the horse. A slug in his rump won't hurt an Indian pony much."

The Pony Soldiers had beaten off the last ride by, and now the Comanche bunched just out of range and talked things over. Once more they streamed past at about fifty yards. When fewer shots came from the brush and logs, the Comanche surged closer. They were met at thirty yards with a barrage of hot army lead. Two more braves were picked off their horses and fell dead to the ground. Three more horses died in their charge.

The Comanche hurriedly pulled back.

"Seven," Captain Kenny said softly. They had killed seven of the Comanche and put at least ten of their ponies out of action.

As he watched the gathering of savages, two of them broke away and rode toward the creek. They entered the area of tall dry grass two hundred yards upstream and a moment later rode out of the grass.

Smoke sifted up, then billowed in a black cloud as the wind pushed the just set fire toward the hidden cavalrymen along the stream. The fire ran before the wind, jumped the creek and raced down the far side. For a while it looked at if the fire would go around them, then it turned with the wind and raced toward them.

"Into the creek!" Captain Kenny bellowed. "Lie down, get wet all over. If the fire gets to us, we run out the other side and get our horses!"

The men moved to the foot deep creek and lay down, soaking their pants and shirts, spilling hatfulls of water over their heads.

The fire boiled toward them, but when it was twenty yards away, the crazy Texas wind shifted again and blew the flames back on themselves into the charred grass. The fire went out.

"Back to the logs!" Kenny yelled. "Here they come again."

The fire had blackened a large area to the left of the cavalrymen and prevented the Comanches from sneaking up on them through the grass that had been there.

It was a frontal attack again, riding by, screaming and firing from under the pony's neck. Two more ponies were killed and the men on foot were quickly picked up by the charging horsemen and ridden to the rear out of danger.

Two more of his men had been hit, one seriously. Captain Kenny watched the hostiles. They seemed to be arguing among themselves. Two riders rushed forward on their mounts, picked up the two dead or wounded braves and hurried away. Captain Kenny ordered his men not to shoot at the mercy mission.

He could see one of the braves being tied onto a

pony, his hands and feet bound together under the horse's belly.

When the Comanche came toward them the next time, only half rode the circle firing at them. Three or four slid into the brush above and below their position and dismounted. The Indians were coming at them through the brush as well! They would have to defend three sides and at the same time protect their horses.

Captain Kenny yelled at the men, told them of the danger and they hurriedly formed themsleves into a small circle, each man facing outward, so they could defend every point of the compass.

Ten minutes later a shot sounded from the brush upstream. Private Ingles who had been wounded on the first charge took another Comanche bullet. He had been hurting so badly that they couldn't move him. He lay ten feet from the circle.

At once two rifles blasted six rounds into the brushy area where the soft blue smoke rose from the shot. They heard no response.

Captain Kenny scanned the woods in front of him. He put his most experienced men to cover the woods, the two recruits to fire at the horsemen in the open.

Another single shot sounded from downstream. One of the cavalrymen swore.

"Missed me, you bastard!" he shouted and fired six rounds into the brush. A scream billowed from the brush and they could hear someone rushing away.

This time the charge from the mounted savages came within ten yards of the woods before all eight guns left firing cut into the attackers and drove them back.

One more charge like that and we won't be able to fight them off, Kenny thought. He wondered how the ammunition was holding out.

"Conserve your rounds," he barked. "Make every shot count." Captain Kenny counted his rounds. He loaded another magazine tube with the .52 caliber cartridges and lay it beside his Spencer. He had fourteen rounds left. Enough for two more charges, if he was careful. Then he would use his pistol. He should have sixty rounds for the six shooter, but he desperately hoped that the savages didn't get so close he could use the revolver.

A half hour later they had. Four more charges had cut down the captain's effective cavalrymen to four. One had an arrow wound in his left shoulder. The tip had gone all the way through and one of the men had broken the arrow and pulled the shaft out.

Now four of the savages were in the brush to their left close enough for pistol use. He had sent ten rounds at them. There were at least four or five more in the brush on their right, and the mounted Comanches kept riding at them, trying to overrun the position.

"Here they come again!" one of the wounded men shouted. He lay on his back, with an arrow in his upper chest. He hadn't been spitting blood so they figured it had missed his lung.

The devils slashed in on their ponies. Ten of the animals were dead just beyond the brush now. Captain Kenny had no idea why these Comanche were willing to pay such a high price for this one stretch of creek bed.

"One more time!" the captain bellowed. "Let's beat the bastards back once more!"

The dozen mounted Comanche came at them again.

Captain Kenny saw another of his men go down. God! He wasn't sure they could hold out this time.

Just before the Comanche riders charged into the woods to try to overrun them, a cavalry bugle sounded loud and clear from close by blowing the attack call!

To the left and slightly upstream Captain Kenny saw the blue shirts coming. It had to be Sgt. Franklin's squad. The twelve mounted men surged forward, rifles spitting lead. The dozen Comanche raiders stopped, yelled among themselves for a moment, then turned and raced back to where their wounded and dead were on horses.

They paused briefly to exchange rounds with the new detail of yellow legs, then mounted up and charged away into the rolling hills.

The Indians still in the woods, faded away through the brush, both up and downstream. They evidently found where they had left their ponies, mounted and rode after their brothers.

Sgt. Franklin did not make the mistake of splitting his own force and sending half of them chasing the Redskins. He would have ridden into a trap if he had, Captain Kenny figured.

The first squad rode into the woods, dismounted and quickly began to tend to the wounded. Captain Kenny put out guards, then checked his men.

Pvt. English and two other troopers lay dead of arrow and ball. Five more were wounded, but they all could ride. Only three men of the second squad were not casualties.

The sun was fast fading. It would be dark in a half hour.

"We'll camp just upstream tonight," Captain Kenny said. "We'll ride for the fort with first light. These wounded men need to be treated."

Just after dark the three cavalrymen were buried in shallow graves. First squad had an issue small folding shovel that the men took turns using. When the graves were three feet deep, Captain Kenny read a page from his well worn officer's manual. He used the order of burial in the field.

Three men from the first squad stood guard during the night in three hour watches. No Comanche raiders bothered them.

The next morning Captain Kenny counted dead war ponies. There were twelve of them down and dead or dying. He put two out of their misery, picked up two Comanche bows with their strange sinew strings, and half a dozen Comanche war arrows, with their broad metal points, feathers, and the different painted markings on the shafts. He marveled how they could get the shafts so straight without woodworking tools.

They rode for Fort Comfort at six A.M. and arrived shortly before noon. The doctor tended to the wounded at once. Captain Kenny insisted that his men be treated before he was, and watched the doctor work.

That evening as he sat in his favorite chair and smoked his pipe, Pamela came in, her eyes wide in wonder as she looked at the Indian bows and arrows.

"They actually shot you with one of these, Father?"

"Afraid so, I forgot to duck once."

"Savages, they simply are savages."

"Gregory is quite a man, Pamela. He rode to get the other half of our patrol and saved all of our skins. If it hadn't been for him, you'd be going to my funeral tomorrow."

"Oh? Really."

"Yes, really. What I'm saying is that I'm giving him permission to court you."

"That's nice."

"Nice? Before you threatened to tell Captain Harding about my little fight with Gregory if I didn't say he could court you."

"Yes, but now it doesn't seem so important. I was talking to Lieutenant Edwards today. Did you know that he had two years of Harvard before the war? He's really an extremely interesting man."

Captain Kenny frowned, they started to jump up. The pain in his shoulder stopped his quick movement.

"Pamela Kenny, Edwards is also a *married man*. I absolutely refuse to let you see him again, even socially. You forget any silly romantic ideas you might have had about him, do I make this all clear, Pamela?"

"Yes, Father. Of course. You're a wounded army hero. How could I possibly go against what you say? Is there anything I can get for you? Anything I can bring you?"

Captain Kenny frowned at such unusual behavior. She was up to something, just what he would have to find out. Nothing would sink his chances on this base as quickly as his daughter getting mixed up with a married officer.

He sent her for a cold bottle of beer from the sutler's store. Captain Kenny shook his head.

No, it couldn't be. She wasn't crazy enough to become involved with a married officer. It must be something else.

13

Captain Colt Harding and Lt. Riddle sat in the office looking through the dispatches that just came in by two riders from Austin. Since the Wagon Wheel Massacre four months ago, all of the dispatch riders traveled in pairs from Austin.

None had been lost since they doubled up.

"Be damned, look at this," Colt said, flipping a dispatch to Lt. Riddle. He read it.

"From: Col. Phil Sparkman, commanding, Texas Department, San Antonio Texas, Military Division of the Missouri.

"To: Captain Colt Harding, commanding, Fort Comfort, Texas.

"Captain. Reread your suggestion about cold weather gear for winter operations against the Comanche. I have passed your suggestions on to General Phil Sheridan at his headquarters at Chicago of the Military Division of the Missouri.

"Trust he will appreciate them as much as I do.

"While a fort commander has a certain amount of discretionary use of his troops, you are expected to carry out the routine patrols and escort and other duties expected of you.

"Outside of that, I'll be interested in this Lightning Company you have established, and will watch your dispatches for its successes.

"Winter gear. We have almost none. Suggest you issue double blouses and trousers, three times as many socks and obtain any available great coats for your operations. Will inquire further for special cold weather outer garments at once.

Keep me informed."

It was signed: Sparkman.

"I'll be damned. You got some attention from the old man in San Antonio."

"For a minute at least. He'll forget about it before he sends the dispatch. Anything else I need to see?"

"No. At least not until I go through them again."

"How are the homesteaders doing?"

"We send a patrol out past their places every day now, no contact, just to let them know we're in the area. They seem to appreciate it."

"Wilson been in?"

"Nope. Hard at work on his house. Winter is coming fast."

"They won't make it before the freeze. They'll have to do soddies for this winter. Either that or we'll have to house them here. Let's ride out and see Wilson."

They left just after the midday meal. It was a fine little valley, big enough for the five homesteaders if nobody got greedy. They had laid it out well, with the five houses within thirty yards of one another in a rough circle.

The first row of adobe blocks was up but that

was about all. Captain Harding and Lt. Riddle rode into the circle of foundations and found the five men talking near one wagon. Josh Wilson looked up and waved.

"Is there a problem?" Captain Harding asked as he walked his big black over to the gathering.

"Considerable," one man snapped. "The sun ain't warm enough to dry out the damned mud bricks."

"Captain, meet Dominic Franchette, farmer by trade," Wilson said. "Dom is not a bricklayer. Dominic, this is Captain Colt Harding."

They nodded.

"Mr. Franchetti is right. The weather has turned. We might not see more than six or eight more drying days until the first good freeze."

"About decided the same thing, Captain," Wilson admitted. "What the hell are we supposed to do now?"

"Soddy. Build yourselves soddy houses for the winter. Get a good start on your adobe blocks next spring and have your houses finished before midsummer."

"You want us to live in a hole in the ground?" Franchetti asked, anger tingeing his words.

"Not exactly a hole in the ground, Mr. Franchetti. The idea is to start it against a small hill or a bank. Dig into the bank say three feet down. Then cut sod about the size of your adobe blocks and stack them up like bricks. Go into the bank three feet and up three feet and you have a six-foot-high structure.

"Then put the logs across the top, add anything you have to make it waterproof and then put sod on top and a foot of dirt, then more sod and you have a place you can keep warm. I've seen some soddies that would be hard to tell from a frame house once you're inside them."

"Don't want to live in a damned hole," Franchetti said, scowling.

"Mr. Franchetti, I don't know where you come from, but this is Texas. It gets freezing cold here in the winter, and living in that covered wagon is going to mean you'll lose half of your family to pneumonia or maybe just freeze to death. What do the rest of you think about soddies?"

Wilson introduced the other three men.

Harding got down from the saddle and shook hands.

Henry Zigler was about forty, had a wife and seven kids. He was a plodder, a follower. He was the second farmer in the group.

Bert Banning was a rancher. He was a raw-boned Texan by his accent, not over twenty-five or six, had a wife and one child.

Juan Martinez was about the same age as Banning and they appeared to be good friends. He said he was starting a cattle ranch too, and had four sons and a daughter to help him.

Banning took off a low-crowned brown cowboy hat and scratched his light colored hair. "Hell, sounds good to me. Get us out of the damned wind and the cold. Maybe even snow. Can't do nothing else until spring nohow."

The other two men nodded their agreement. To the left a quarter of a mile a series of small hills and ravines and some washes funneled into the valley.

"What about the spot?" Harding asked. "You want to go over to them breaks, or do it right here? You've got plenty of sod around here to build a hundred soddies."

"Let's do it here," Wilson decided. "I'm gonna dig down about two feet, then start stacking up the sod. We can get poles from the creek brush to cover over a twelve-foot span no trouble. Make a twelve by twelve should be big enough."

"Too big," Martinez said. "Lots of work. I'm making mine eight by twelve."

The other men began talking, figuring out how to make windows, where to put the doors, which way to face the house. They soon decided to make the dugout soddy next to their permanent house.

Wilson held out his hand to Captain Harding.

"Thanks for the help. We'd be freezing our balls off out here in another two months."

"Just covering my area of responsibility for civilians," Harding said formally. Then he laughed. "You get started and need help on the sod, you give me a call."

Wilson looked up, pleased. "Obliged, Captain, I'll do that."

"What outfit in the Second were you with, Wilson?"

"Second Battalion, A Company."

"You were an officer?" Riddle asked.

Wilson grinned. "Yeah. Strange times. From corporal to Brevet Captain in six months. We had some powerful bad fights with the Comanches about then, lost most of Company A in two quick battles with the Comanche." He shrugged. "I better get to marking out my new house and digging my basement. Thanks again, Captain."

As they rode back to the fort, Captain Harding nodded. "I think they'll make it. In two days check to see that they have a good start, then send out two squads to help them cut out sod. If they don't get those soddies up, we'll have thirty-two more mouths to feed and bodies to house inside the fort.''

Lt. Riddle looked at his captain. "Right. We've got enough problems with our own. Speaking of trouble, has our Miss Pamela been behaving herself lately?"

"Far as I know. October can't come too quickly for me when she'll be gone."

The same time the captain rode back from his talk with the homesteaders, Pamela was thinking about Second Lieutenant Ned Young. She had been trying for three days to get him alone, and at last she figured out how to do it.

There were two unoccupied officer quarters along the officer's country side of the fort. One of the doors had been left unlocked and Pamela discovered it.

Twice she had met Lt. Young on the fort. She had smiled sweetly and made some excuse to talk to him. Each time she had told him she thought he was the very finest officer at the fort, and that he was dashing and handsome in his uniform. She had promised a lot with her eyes when she left.

Now she had the spot where they could talk, alone, if only she could find Lt. Young. She had figured out how she could do it. She combed out her hair, put on a bonnet and asked her mother if she could go to the sutler's store for some blue thread. Her mother frowned but nodded.

"You come right back and don't be talking to anybody, you hear?"

Pamela hurried out the door, walked the long way around the square past the barracks and enjoyed the men staring at her. Nobody knew about her kissing Cpl. Gregory, and they never would. At the sutler's store she bought some blue thread. Lt. Young was not there. She went home past the unfinished section of the fort and saw a work party there. Lt. Young was directing them.

He saw her and came to the edge of the new building.

"Miss Kenny. Afternoon. It's warmed up a little."

"Yes, Ned, it has. Could you help me. I have a problem."

He looked at her quickly.

"I know, we can't talk here. The second officers quarters down from ours are vacant, the door is unlocked. Could I see you there at four-thirty? I would be just ever so grateful."

Lt. Young watched her with critical blue eyes. He was five feet nine inches tall, about average for the day, with soft brown hair he kept cut short. He had a closely trimmed moustache.

"Is this something really important, Pamela?"

"Yes! Oh, yes! It's military, officer-enlisted man thing, and I need an officer's advice."

He half turned away. "Yes, I'll be there. Just don't let anyone see you go in." He walked away as if they hadn't been talking at all.

Pamela grinned. She felt a little stirring way down deep between her legs and her face blossomed into a big smile. Two enlisted men walking by, noticed, and turned to watch her.

At twenty minutes after four, Pamela convinced her mother she had the wrong shade of blue thread and left for the sutler's store to exchange it. She knew this was a busy time around the fort. Men were working with their horses after exercises or training. The enlisted men were still under orders and busy.

She walked slowly along the path under the awnings along officer row. At the vacant quarters she simply turned the knob and went inside. Anyone seeing her would mistakenly suppose that was her father's quarters.

The inside was chilly, the government issued furniture stark and some covered with sheets. She pulled the sheet off a couch and sat down to wait. For a moment her hand rubbed her left breast and she smiled. There would be no problem with Lt. Young, she was sure. She remembered pressing against his leg at supper at her father's quarters. He hadn't really removed her leg. Somehow his wife had known what she was doing. The bitch!

The door opened and Lt. Young stepped inside. He pushed the locking bolt in softly and turned to her.

"I don't want anybody surprising us and getting the wrong idea. This is strictly officer advice, friendly, impersonal. You know I'm married. There can never be anything—"

When he turned around, Pamela had the top of her dress open and spread apart. She wore no chemise or wrapper under it. Lt. Young had taken two steps toward her before he saw her. Her big breasts glowed with their youth, all milky white with soft pink areolas and deep red, large nipples.

Ned Young took another step and stopped. She jumped up and threw her arms around him, pressing her bare breasts against him.

"Darling Ned! I've wanted you to make love to me since the moment I saw you! You're the handsomest man I've ever seen." She leaned back. "Do you like my titties?"

Lt. Young groaned. His wife had been cold as

an icicle lately. He always had been fascinated by breasts. His hand came up and covered one. They were so big, so beautiful!

"Yes, darling! Pet them. They want you to pet them. Oh, that is marvelous. You can do just *anything* you want to me, lover. Anything, but we've got to hurry."

Fifteen minutes later, Lt. Young pulled up blue pants with the yellow stripe down the leg. Christ, twice in fifteen minutes! He still didn't believe it. She was so young, and beautiful, and she'd let him do anything. She had let him make love to her the one way he'd always wanted to try.

Neither of them had fully undressed. She pulled her dress together and buttoned it. When she stood Lt. Young couldn't tell she wore nothing under it. Not a damn thing!

He went to the door and cracked it open and looked out. "You go first. I'll wait awhile. I can always say I'm thinking about changing quarters."

Pamela slipped out to the walk in front of the rooms and went quickly back toward her parent's quarters. In her pocket was the same spool of thread, but she'd convince her mother it was a different shade.

The flush had faded from her cheeks. What a lover! Lt. Young was going to be the best serviced officer in the army. Now she knew it would be easy to be with him again. Her whole body warmed as she thought about their love-making.

Then she pushed it out of her mind as she went through the door and into her parent's place. She had to play the dutiful daughter again—for awhile!

* * *

At the homesteader's site, the five men were digging. Each one had laid down chalk lines for the inside measurements of his soddy house. The more they worked the smaller the temporary house became. At last they all decided to build soddies that were ten feet square.

Josh Wilson had spaded down a foot deep around his ten foot perimeter. It was hard work. He dug methodically. None of them came out here expecting sudden riches and luxury. They just hadn't thought about housing for the first winter. Josh realized they had started too late in the summer. But they all had the land they wanted, and had a start on their houses.

They talked about all working on one soddy at a time, but first they had to get started. There were no hired hands available. Josh's wife, Mary, came out of their covered wagon, and smiled, the edges of weariness showing through. She had been a city girl in St. Louis. He'd warned her about marrying him, but she wouldn't let him go.

She was of sturdy German stock, and larger than most women at five feet five. She took a round pointed shovel from near the wagon and stepped over the chalk line.

"Welcome to my living room," she said, then began to throw dirt out of the hole and far enough to the side to leave space for the twelve-inch-wide sod strips they would be laying down the walls.

By sundown, Mary had blisters on her right hand.

"Darn, I forgot to give you gloves," Josh said. They paused and looked at their new home. They were down a foot and a half in one corner, over a foot around the rest of it. They put down their tools and went to check on the Martinez soddy.

Juan grinned up at them. Juan, Carmelita and their two oldest boys all were throwing dirt out of the hole. Juan had a square pointed shovel and leveled out the bottom two feet down. Half of the ten foot square was down to depth, the rest nearly so.

"We'll come help you as soon as we get ours dug," Juan said. "We help each other, just like we planned in Austin."

"Damn right, Juan!" Josh said quickly. "You've got some mighty good dirt diggers there."

Carmelita looked at the sun. "Supper!" she said and dropped her shovel.

"Me, too," Mary Wilson said and hurried back to her wagon to light a cooking fire and get some food ready. She wasn't sure what to have tonight. There were leftover baked beans from dinner, and she would boil some potatoes. She also boiled some beef jerky they had brought with them. It wasn't bad when it was boiled up and then fried.

Josh grabbed Carmelita's shovel and began digging. He and Juan talked about how they would start their roundups in the spring. They would bring the cattle into a small valley just downstream about two miles. They could herd them in the small valley until they got used to staying together.

All three of the men had registered brands with the state at Austin before they left. They even had a blacksmith make up two branding irons each for them. Josh had his brand the JW. He was getting anxious to brand his first cow, but that would not be until spring.

After they got their soddies up, the men

planned to ride south and east looking for cattle. They could rope a dozen or so and drive them back to their ranches. The beef would be their main staple of food during the winter. Any of the cows that survived would be the start of their herd.

"Figure we can round up about twenty, maybe twenty-five before the snow flies," Juan said.

As they finished cleaning up the bottom of the square, it was dusk.

"Be over to help you tomorrow," Juan said as the men waved and went to their wagons and the warmth of their campfires.

Josh took a cup of coffee Mary handed him and sat down next to the larger fire away from the cooking fire that glowed with hot coals but little flame.

"Yes, Mary, we were right in coming. I'm glad we did. We have a chance to build something good out here. If the damn Comanches stay their distance until we get established and can afford some ranch hands who will be guards too, we should be all right."

Mary watched their three children, ages five to one, playing in the covered wagon.

"I know it's going to work out, Josh. We'll work hard and hope for the best. What else can we do? I know it's going to be just fine."

14

Pamela Kenny sat in her room on the big bed patiently working on a cross stitch napkin. It was supposed to be a set of four, a Christmas present for her aunt in Boston, but that had been for last Christmas. Maybe next Christmas.

She smiled to herself, glowing at the gentle way Lt. Ned Young had made love to her. She was a woman! She could take care of a man's needs just as well as any woman. Probably a lot better. Ned said they did it a way he had never done before! She was so thrilled and delighted! Maybe she should marry Ned after all.

He was an officer. She giggled. She didn't care a twit about whether a man was an officer or enlisted. She thought the whole army thing was just stupid and silly and loved it when she and her mother could live off a post in the city. Like in San Antonio, even. It had been better in Washington. Now she would give her girdle to live in Washington D.C.!

She laughed softly. There were plans to be made. She would carry on her affair with Ned for another month, then insist that he divorce his wife and marry her. It was the only right thing he could do, the proper thing.

Pamela laughed again. Men were so ridiculous. Didn't they think women enjoyed sex as much as they did? They were silly fools, but women had to put up with them. They were needed around a bedroom.

"Pamela." Her mother called. "I need you to help me get dinner ready. Come on out here."

Pamela checked with a hand mirror to make sure she was not flushed, then she went out and peeled potatoes and carrots to go in the beef stew her mother had cooking.

It was a little after noon the next day when Pamela made another trip to the sutler's for a bright red yarn for the cross stitchery work. She had some but her mother didn't know it. There was a chance she might run into Lt. Young.

He wasn't in the store, but the minute Pamela entered the roughly set out establishment, she realized that Grace Young, Lt. Young's wife, was there.

The woman who had cried and yelped and hurried away at the dinner a few weeks before, did not run away this time. She marched up to Pamela and without warning slapped her face.

Pamela jumped back a foot, her eyes wide, a startled yelp sputtering from her mouth.

"What in the world?" Pamela said.

"You know precisely what that was for. Should I do it again?"

Pamela looked at Grace Young, and this time spoke softly so no one else could hear.

"If you can't hold your husband, that's your problem."

Grace Young surged forwrd, her eyes furious, her mouth open in a yell of hatred, her fingernails clawing at Pamela's face. The younger girl tried to jump away, but Mrs. Young was determined.

She grabbed Pamela with one hand and her fingernails raked down across Pamela's face, digging four deep grooves in her cheeks, which filled with blood.

Pamela screamed. But she didn't retreat. She lashed out with her reticule, banging Grace on the side of the head. Then Pamela rushed forward her fist doubled up, her right arm stiff. It was more of a battering ram than a punch, but it connected with Grace Young's jaw and knocked her down.

Grace sat down with a plop, and Pamela fell on top of her, screeching and clawing and pulling her hair. The two rolled over in the aisle, dumping a stack of galvanized buckets.

Mr. Altzanger, the store manager, rushed up.

"Stop that! Ladies, stop that at once!" he shouted.

The two women on the floor rolled over again. Grace Young hit Pamela with her closed fist and Pamela's nose spouted a red flood.

Pamela kicked Grace off and sat up, clawed at Grace's face. This time her fingers found flesh and drew two bloody trails down the woman's cheeks. Grace screamed and dove forward, her head hitting Pamela's chest and driving her to the floor.

A pair of enlisted men looked on with glee, cheering on the two fighters.

Sgt. Casemore happened in the store and he ran up, grabbed Pamela and shouted for Altzanger to hold Mrs. Young. A moment later the women were parted, both still on the floor. Their skirts hiked up over their knees, exposing legs encased in stockings and white drawers.

"Ladies, cover yourselves!" Altzanger said in a hushed whisper. The six enlisted men watching cheered, then booed when the skirts covered up the women.

"You two better get back to your quarters," Altzanger said, mopping his suddenly sweaty brow. A captain's daughter and a lieutenant's woman! It would be all over the fort in ten minutes.

Sgt. Casemore looked sternly at Pamela. "Your father is going to be unhappy about this," he said. "I better see that you get back to your quarters." He reached down to help Pamela up. Instead of reaching for his hand, she swung her fist once more, catching Grace on the right eye.

Sgt. Casemore grabbed her hand, pulled her to her feet and propelled her out the door to the sidewalk. Mrs. Young would have a beaut of a shiner come morning.

"You shouldn't be fighting," Sgt. Casemore said as he held her arm and walked her quickly toward her quarters.

"The bitch insulted me!" Pamela snorted. "And she hit me first."

"I don't know how your father is going to react, but I do know what Captain Harding will do. You could even wind up in the stockade."

"He wouldn't!"

"Matter of discipline. Be surprised what can happen." He knocked on the door and waited until Mrs. Kenny opened it. She took one look at Pamela and thrust her fists to her hips.

"Now you've done it, girl. You'll be in Austin within two days if I know the army and your father. Then to Boston with you. My poor sister doesn't know what she's asking for."

"Then don't tell her, Mama. Sergeant, would you ask the fort doctor to come treat my wounds? I might catch rabies from that mad animal that attacked me."

Sgt. Casemore touched his hat in a salute. "Yes, Miss, I'll be glad too. She's all yours, Mrs. Kenny. Fracas took place down at the store with Mrs. Young."

Ruth Kenny nodded and pulled Pamela inside. The door closed promptly and there was a loud wail through it as Sgt. Casemore walked across the parade toward the fort medical office.

Captain Kenny heard about the fight within fifteen minutes of the last round. He left his small company office and marched straight across the parade grounds to his quarters. Doc Jenkins had just finished tending to Pamela. He had put some antiseptic on the scratches and applied a cold cloth to her nose to stop the bleeding. Then he put salve on the scrapes.

"Captain. Got the wounded all tended to. Broke up my day something fine. The scratches aren't deep enough to leave scars, but there will be a thin mark there for six months or so."

"Thanks, Captain, I appreciate your professional ministrations." He pointed to Pamela and motioned her into the kitchen.

Ruth Kenny let the doctor out and he rubbed his jaw as he left, paused a minute looking at the closed door, and then chuckled as he walked back across the parade to his small dispensary.

He should retire from the army, set himself up in a nice little practice for rich old ladies in Chicago, and live out his days with fine food, fine music and drama, and get waited on hand and foot by his wife. Should do it, probably never would.

Inside the Kenny quarters, Captain Kenny stared in frustration at his only offspring.

"How could you do something like this, Pamela?"

"Me do it? She slapped me first, right there in the store. I just came in to get some yarn and she walked right up to me and slapped me and started hitting and scratching me, and—"

Captain Kenny held up his hand stopping her.

"There's more to it than that. Why did she hit you?"

"I don't have the slightest idea. The woman must be unstable, a real crazy."

"No, she isn't. What did you do, Pamela?"

"I didn't do anything! I don't know why she hit me. I didn't do a blamed thing!" She ran out of the room to her big bed and slammed the door.

A half hour later, Captain Kenny was back in his quarters after a frank talk with Lt. Young and his wife. He went to see Pamela in her room.

"You'll be leaving the fort day after tomorrow, Pamela. I've checked with Captain Harding. You and your mother will go on the supply wagon to Austin. There will be a twenty man escort. From there you and your mother will go to Boston. Your mother will explain in detail the trouble you've been in here, with Lieutenant Young and with Corporal Gregory.

"Your aunt is a strict woman. You won't have a chance to stray from the straight and narrow there. The matter is closed."

At seven-thirty the next morning, Captain Harding rode out of Fort Comfort with his forty man Lightning Company. They were rigged for the field, three days rations, one blanket, one change of shirt and socks, their rifle and pistol.

They rode past the homesteaders and found two squads of men from C Company under Lt. Young's direction, cutting sod from the prairie and hauling it in flat bed wagons to the five soddy houses which were progressing nicely. One was up to window level, a second one up to head height and a dozen poles had been stretched across to start the roof.

Captain Harding turned the men into the next valley over where he called them around him.

"You're in advanced training now, men. First our review. We'll have a competition on the pickup of a downed rider." He laid out the course. The squads competed against each other. All of the squads except one man dismounted. The contest was to pick up a downed rider, and bring him back to the starting line, where a second rider would leave, go out and pick up the next downed man until the entire squad had picked up a rider and been picked up himself.

Second squad won the match.

They moved on to shooting at a dummy target by firing under the horse's neck. One man fell off, and was teased by every other man in the company. When each man had fired five rounds at the target under the mount's neck, Captain Harding called them together again.

"You all have knives. Some we issue, some you buy. Just how well you can use that weapon could save your hide. The Comanche are expert knife fighters. And the Tonkawas aren't slouches. We have four Tonks to give us some pointers. Break up into squads and do the knife training."

The men grumbled. Captain Harding bristled.

"You'd rather sit on your ass back at the fort and get your fat ass shot off the next time we go out on patrol? If not, sharpen up! You'll be using sticks instead of knives so nobody gets killed. Watch these Tonks, they know knives. Let's do it!"

The Tonkawa Indians called out one man at a time, and gave him a stick for a knife. Then they invited the tropper to attack them. Nine times out of ten, the Tonkawa would disarm the trooper and have his stick knife at the blue shirt's throat.

Patiently the Tonkawas drilled into men the basics of fighting with a knife: Stay low, use it to slash or stab. Never let the other man know what you will do in advance. Protect yourself. Always be ready to take a wound on your arm or shoulder to get inside and give a fatal thrust or slash of your own.

Sgt. Casemore growled and charged his Tonkawa. He had done some knife fighting for real, but the Tonk sidestepped his charge, tripped him, kicked away his stick knife and held his own stick across Sgt. Casemore's throat.

Sgt. Casemore worked for twenty minutes before he was sure he had a better method of knife fighting. He just prayed to God that he never would have to rely on his knife.

Captain called the men together again and they took a dinner break. It was cold and fast. The sun was directly overhead and the only warm thing around. After twenty minutes, Captain Harding told them the next project.

"Designate one man from each squad as the runner. That man will ride out in any direction he wants to go, and have fifteen minutes to get to a hiding spot.

"Then your Tonkawa scout will teach you how to track that man. Once the runner has gone for fifteen minutes he must stay in place until he's found. Don't just follow the scout. He'll make you do most of the work. Look for hoofprints, bent grass, listen for noises, watch for sudden flights of birds or movements of animals. I want every man in this troop to be able to track a midget through a patch of cactus and never get scratched."

Captain Harding made the men face away from the direction the runners took. When they had ridden out of sight, he turned the men around and the tracking lesson began.

The Tonkawas were all good trackers. Captain Harding had learned as much as he could from them on his ten day junket three months ago to find out where Sadie was. Now he wanted his men to know the same things.

The scouts made the men take turns finding the trail. They corrected when the trail was lost, showed why they got off it. When an unusual problem came up, they explained mostly by signs what went wrong, or how to find the way over sheet rock, or down a stream.

All four of the runners were tracked down in an hour. Captain Harding nodded, told Sgt. Casemore to head the men back to camp. They rode in tired, but somehow more pleased with their army duty, and their new found skills, than any of them would have thought possible six months ago.

Captain Harding had his dinner brought to him that night, read a magazine for two hours, then went over his master plan. His troop was ready for the Comanche. He hadn't heard from any travelers lately about where the White Eagle band could be. There had been no more trouble with raiding Comanches since Captain Kenny's attack.

But where was Sadie?

The trader, the halfbreed, who had led them straight to White Eagle's camp, had stayed at the fort for a week. Then he headed for Austin and new supplies. He wouldn't trade with the Indians again until next spring and summer. Nobody else had come through from Indian country.

The Pamela Kenny problem was resolving itself. He didn't have to take a hand in it. Captain Kenny knew what had to be done. Colt fully expected that the girl had bedded Lt. Young somehow, and his wife found out. Young probably would stay at the Fort. The gossip would die down quickly.

Even the homesteaders were shaping up. With another week of good weather, the soddies should be done and the families moved inside. Then they could concentrate on making rock and concrete fireplaces in each soddy. There weren't enough pot bellied heating stoves for all the soddies.

Stoves could be moved out of unused officer quarters, but Captain Harding hoped for the fireplaces.

Sadie, Sadie, Sadie! He took out a bottle of whiskey he had been saving. A knock sounded on his door. He opened it and found Doc Jenkins there.

"Figured it was 'bout time we had another game of chess. What do you say, Captain?"

"You ready to get your ass whipped again, Jenkins?"

"Mmmmmm. Never ready for that, but has happened. Cán't rightly remember when. Back in twenty-eight as I recall."

They both laughed and the doctor came in and set up the board he carried under his arm.

They played four games of chess, each winning two. By the time the doctor went home, the bottle of whiskey had been reduced by nearly half.

"Good night, sweet prince," Doc Jenkins said and weaved into the night.

Captain Harding was sober as a Comanche tee-totaler. That bothered him a little. He was still trying to come up with an absolutely unstoppable way to rescue Sadie as he fell asleep.

15

The lookout in the fort's tower near the front gate saw him first. There was only a thin trail of dust followed by a larger dust trail. The sergeant of the guard reported to the officer of the day, Lt. Edwards, who sent out a six man patrol to investigate.

'Yes sir, Captain,'' Lt. Edwards reported minutes after the patrol went out. "It looked damn like a small force, maybe six or eight, chasing one rider.''

Both officers went to the lookout and used their field glasses. By then the dust trails were closer. The Pony Soldiers were a mile out and riding hard.

"Damn, I think you're right, Edwards. Looks like one rider with about six Comanches riding hell to leather behind him. The Indians only have one pony each, which is probably why the rider in front still has his scalp.''

They heard rifle fire then. At a half mile the patrol began firing in the direction of the chasers. There was little chance to hit them, but the pursuit group hesitated, came on another hundred yards, then turned and rode off.

"I gave Sergeant Barlow instructions not to chase the hostiles if they were Comanche," Lt. Edwards said. They watched the patrol meet with the lone rider, turn and escort him back toward the fort at a walk.

"I want to talk to that man when he gets in and recuperates a little," Captain Harding said as he went down the ladder to the fort roof, then to the ground. "Wonder where in hell those Comanches came from?"

An hour later Lt. Edwards brought a man into Captain Harding's office. He was short, stocky and looked tough as saddle leather. He had a full beard, at least six months worth, and his brown eyes glittered from under bushy eyebrows. The man wore store bought jeans and a homemade fringed buckskin shirt. He stepped forward briskly and held out his hand. Colt guessed he was not thirty yet.

"Want to thank you and your men, Captain. Damn hostiles was againing on me at the last there."

"I'm Captain Harding, glad we could help."

"Oh, my moniker is Lars Chaney. Guide covered wagon trains over the Oregon trail. Thought I'd take a look a little farther south coming back this time. Traveling alone."

"How many Comanches chase you?"

"Started with about twenty, I'd say. But they didn't have no spare ponies to switch to, so I figured Sioux Chief and me could outlast them. That is one hell of a horse I got."

"Comanches probably wanted the horse more than they did you," Lt. Edwards said.

"About the size of it. Mighty obliged for the help out there. Nothing like half dozen Pony Soldiers to put the Comanches on the run."

"I wish that were true. How far did they chase you, Mr. Chaney?"

"Well, let's see. They spotted me about ten o'clock yesterday morning. I'd say that was about a hundred and twenty miles out mostly north and a little to the west."

"Your horse ran for a hundred and twenty miles?" Captain Harding asked, incredulous.

"Well, no. I knew Sioux Chief could outlast them little Indian ponies. All I had to do was stay alive. Had this blanket that I doubled over so it was three inches thick and I tied that to my back and so it covered my neck.

"Then I rode. I'd charge along and outdistance the heathens, then old Sioux Chief and me would walk, resting up. When the Indian ponies started catching up within arrow shot distance, Sioux Chief and me would ride hard again and get a big lead."

"And you did that for twenty-four hours?" Lt. Edwards asked.

"Peers as how. Once they knew a short cut I didn't and they damn near got me. But I figured something like that was sprouting, so I didn't walk that time, just kept riding and came out about a quarter of a mile ahead of them. You never seen such a bunch of mad Indians in your whole damn life!"

"Did that blanket stop any arrows?" Lt. Edwards asked. "We found several arrow wounds on your horse."

"Deed it did, Lieutenant. I felt at least a dozen good solid hits. When I'd get ahead I'd reach around and clean them off. I guess six or eight stuck in the blanket."

"You're welcome to stay and rest up, Mr. Chaney," Colt Harding said. "Glad we could be of service. I do want to ask you some questions about your route, when you first saw the savages, if you saw a camp, where it was, then your route here."

"Yep, more than happy. That map will help." He went to the wall map of western Texas and studied it for a minute.

"I go mostly by rivers. I came down around that helluva big caprock out there, this side of it and went mostly south then. Let's see, rivers. Streams." He stared at the map for a minute.

"What are all of these pins and tacks?"

"Those are locations where Comanche bands have camped or hunted," Captain Harding said. "We're trying to keep track of them."

"Oh, well I sure came through a batch of them. Traveled mostly by night and thought I'd slipped through. Then just about here, they spotted me, and the chase began."

"That's at the headwaters of the North Concho River," Captain Harding said. "We've never been in there much. Was it a hunting camp, or set up for winter?"

"Damned if I know. I kept away from their camps as much as I could. Did see a hunt going on at one place."

"Were they big camps or smaller ones?"

"Hunting camps, maybe forty or fifty tipis, in the ones I saw. Half a dozen camps strung between there and the big cap rocks."

"Could you take us back to the spot you last saw the Comanche camps?" Colt Harding asked.

"Sure, for a scout's pay. What can you offer?"

"Pay you a dollar a day. More than a second lieutenant makes in this man's army."

"Done. I get to bring my own horse."

"Done," Colt said and reached out his hand. "We'll be riding in the morning, so rest up." He looked at him. "And eat something, I don't want you falling off your horse half way there."

Cpl. Swenson took the scout out to get him some quarters and food.

Colt looked at Lt. Edwards. "I'll be riding the Lightning Company fast tomorrow. I want your company to follow us at forty miles a day. We've got about a hundred and ten miles to do. You'll be there in three, and we'll be there in two. No wagons. Expect to be in the field for about eight days. Take six Tonkawa scouts. Two for scouts and four to hunt for the troop. We'll move out at six-thirty as usual."

"Yes, sir, I can put forty-eight of my fifty men into the field."

"Good, make it double issue of ammo, and food for eight days issued to each man. Your scouts will know the general area, but have them follow our trail. See you at supper."

Two days later, Captain Harding trailed his column of fours into a sparse growth of live oak on a dry hillside. They had been seeing fragments of a herd of buffalo most of the afternoon. Now just before sunset they came on a herd that stretched more than a mile in front of them.

"I've never seen so many buffalo in one place," Captain Harding told Sgt. Casemore as they stopped and looked out across the shaggy brown mass of animals.

"I'd guess maybe fifty thousand," Sgt. Casemore said. "Damn, they just keep showing up down beyond that hill!"

"Bring up the scouts, let's do some calculating," Captain Harding told his sergeant.

A few minutes later the lead scout, Hatchet, Captain Harding and Sgt. Casemore looked over the top of the small rise to the north. The buffalo herd was only a scattering of brown splotches on that side of the hill. Not more than two miles ahead they could see smoke from a dozen Indian tipis drifting into the windless sky.

"Hunting camp," Hatchet said.

"How many Comanches?" Harding asked.

"Three hands warriors."

"Fifteen," Lt. Edwards said to the scout. He shrugged.

"No chance to slip up on the place in the daylight across all that open land. We'll wait for darkness and be ready to hit them in the morning. I want to know for sure if it's White Eagle's band or not."

They dismounted in the shade of the evergreen leaves of the live oak and waited.

The Lightning Company had quickly left the regular troops behind the first day as they moved away from the fort at a smart canter and with the scout Lars Chaney leading the way. By now they were a day ahead of Company B and Lt. Edwards.

As darkness settled over the high plains, the mass of brown buffalo blended together into a sea, then faded to blackness. They had heard no shots from the hunting camp. Evidently this band used only arrows to kill the big buffalo.

When it was full dark, the troop mounted and rode at a walk down the far side of the small hill and toward the brush lined stream where the

Indians had their hunt camp.

The brush would cover their approach from the down wind side. Captain Harding remembered seeing a small wooden hill slightly north and behind the hunting camp. This was their objective. They circled well around the camp, passed shaggy mounds of buffalo bedded down and sleeping, and at last came to the point where they could ride up the slope into more live oak. A few pecan trees lined the stream course.

Once under cover with his troops, Captain Harding took Sgt. Casemore and Hatchet and worked through the woods as close to the Indians as they thought safe. There were several camp-fires among the tipis but none was large enough to shed much light on the size of the place or the number of people.

Captain Harding could not determine if any of the tipis had a large eagle head painted on it.

Back with the rest of the troop, Captain Harding gave the men four hours of sleep. They put out double guards. Then Colt Harding settled against a tree. They had left their horses saddled to be ready to move or fight at a moment's warning. Colt thought about the upcoming battle. If they were only a small band, he would kill all of the men and destroy the camp, sending the women and children chasing away to a different band. They always seemed to know where the other groups were.

He would not slaughter the women and children. As he dreamed he wondered where Sadie was and how he could rescue her.

Cpl. Swenson touched his shoulder and he came awake, his hand on one of the ivory handled pistols at his hip.

"Yes?"

"Four-thirty, sir, silent reveille," Swenson said.

"Thanks, Swenson, get Sgt. Casemore over here."

Captain Harding wanted to order Hatchet and his Tonkawa scouts to the rear and not engage in the fight, but by the time he sent for them, they had already vanished into the night. They would join the fight when it was won, and escape with some of the loot they prized highest, Comanche steaks.

The Lighting troop mounted up and paused at the fringe of woods along the small creek less than a hundred yards from the sleeping Indian hunting camp.

Faint streaks of light stabbed through the darkness, bursting it apart as dawn came slowly, irreversibly.

With the light, Captain Harding rode up and down the line of troopers staring at the various tipi tops. Nowhere could he find an eagle head. This was not White Eagle's band.

The Pony Soldiers had their orders. They would kill every Indian man they could find. They would not harm the women and children unless one of them fought back with deady force by bow or firearm. Then the trooper would defend himself with deadly force.

As the night gave way to dawn, Colt Harding could see that the tipis were surrounded with racks and racks of meat that would finish drying in the sun. He had seen the racks up close. They had sharpened pegs to stab the meat on. The rows of pegs bound to a bipod on each end and laced across with crossbars. Simple to make, to take down and carry along.

All at once it was fully daylight. A dog barked in the village. A brave lifted a flap and walked towards the brush behind the tipis to relieve himself. Before Colt could designate a man to shoot the warrior, a bowstring twanged and just as the brave looked up, a Tonkawa arrow drove through his chest, killing him without a sound.

Captain Harding lifted one of his ivory handled pistols and waved the men forward. Sgt. Casemore at the far end of the line of forty men spaced five yards apart did the same. When they were out of the brush, Captain Harding doubled his fist and pumped it up and down over his head and the line of men began to run forward.

A pistol shot slammed through the brisk Texas morning jolting the troopers out of their sense of unreality. One of the Pony Soldiers screeched in pain and fell with a round in his shoulder.

The Indian who shot the captured pistol, bellowed a Comanche war cry and was cut down by five .52 caliber Spencer rifle bullets. But the camp was alerted.

Warriors fled their tents with pistols and rifles and bows and arrows. Four of the braves were blasted into Comanche heaven before they could turn and fight. Three more ducked behind other tipis and resisted.

The line of troops kept running, swept through the first line of tipis and caught two braves nocking arrows. They surged around the tents, and when the firing was over outside, two man teams searched each tipi, but found no more men, only women and children.

A young boy of about twelve caught up his dead father's fourteen-foot-long lance with the razor sharp point and rammed it forward at a soldier's broad back. Before he got there two Spencer slugs hit him, knocking him down. The lance missed, and the Indian boy died.

After a brief talk with the captain, Sgt. Casemore told his men to herd all of the people to the far end of the camp and make them sit down on the grass.

When that was done six men went through the village with torches, setting everything on fire that would burn. The rest of the drying racks were knocked down, and thrown on the burning tipis.

The wranglers brought up the horses where they had been kept safe, and half the troops mounted while the other half pushed over tipis so they would burn faster, and piled unburned poles into the flames to be sure they were destroyed.

Rawhide boxes of jerky were thrown into the flames. Everything they could find that would burn was destroyed. Just as they were about to mount up the rest of the troop, a single war pony thundered into the camp from the woods. The brave on the horse saw the devastation, wheeled his horse and amid a dozen shots, fled back into the brush.

"Two men! Follow him! Don't let him get away alive!" Sgt. Casemore had bellowed the command without asking his captain. Two men closest to the man surged after him on their black army mounts.

"Let's get out of here to some defensible spot, Sergeant," Captain Harding called. The troop mounted up, rode into the bush and back to the small knoll where they had spent the night.

On the long flat land extending from the small hill, they could see three horses racing north. One of the horses faded and soon stopped. The second man fired a full magazine of rounds at the Indian ahead of him, but he was soon a quarter of a mile ahead and out of effective range.

Slowly the last pursuer turned and rode back. A messenger had escaped.

When the two riders returned, Sgt. Casemore and Captain Harding had decided.

"No sense waiting for whoever he's going to tell what he saw and bring them back. We've finished our mission, let's move toward the fort on our trail coming out so we'll meet Lieutenant Edwards."

They rode at their usual sixty-five mile pace, and it was just before noon that they saw the first hostiles. A lone Indian brave silhouetted himself on a small hill to the left of the line of march and waited until he was sure the Pony Soldiers saw him. Then he slid down out of site behind the hill.

"Trouble," Sgt. Casemore said, riding up to his captain.

"I saw him. What do we have around here for a defensive position if we need one?"

"Not a damn thing, Captain."

"Pull in our outriders. Those damn Tonks back from their feast yet?"

"Not a chance. That's a two day pig-out for them," Sgt. Casemore said.

"Look up there, Sergeant."

Then men both looked ahead. A small valley opened up and from it rode thirty Comanche warriors, painted, armed and ready to do battle.

"Thirty of them, forty of us, not bad odds," Casemore said. "None of that last bunch had many rifles. If all they got is bows and arrows, we won't have any trouble."

They heard a scream behind them, and racing toward them a quarter of a mile away came a cloud of Indians.

"Christ! Must be a hundred of them!" Colt bellowed. He looked around again. The small stream was wider here. Just ahead he saw an island where the water swept around each side. It was twenty yards wide and three times that long. More important, it was thick with wild pecan trees and a few live oak. It might be just enough of an advantage.

"To the island!" Captain Harding bellowed. The troops saw it and galloped fifty yards to it, splashing through two-foot-deep water to get to the dry land in the middle. The wrangler grabbed the horses and moved them to the center of the little island and tied them individually to trees.

Quickly the troopers dropped behind trees and a few logs. Some began piling up rocks at the very front of the "V" where the water parted to go around the island.

"How many of them would you guess?" Sgt. Casemore asked, his voice calm.

"At least a hundred and fifty," Colt said. "I should have figured it. Such a large herd of buffalo would pull in the Comanche from all over the surrounding area this time of the year. They're having their last hunt before their winter camp."

The rushing Comanches from the rear had stopped two hundred yards away. They had not expected a pitched battle. They wanted to ride down the yellow legs horse to horse, lance against pistol. This was not an expected move by a cavalry unit.

The Indians from the front of them swept

around one side, out of effective rifle range and teamed with the hostiles upstream.

"Keep your heads down men, and let's find out what they have. My guess they are short on rifles. They wanted to get in close where their lances and bows and arrows are more deadly. We'll find out soon."

Sgt. Casemore had moved half way down on one side of the double line of troopers. He had stretched them at four yard intervals from the point down each side, then put two men in the middle.

"Make yourselves any kind of barricade you can," Casemore bellowed. "Old logs, rocks. Use your cup to dig up rocks and dirt. You beat that cup up enough right here saving your scalp, you'll be glad to drink from it all scratched and bent."

As the soldiers waited, the Indians milled around. Now and then one or two would gallop flat out toward the Pony Soldiers, only to pull up and spin around and race away.

There seemed to be some kind of discussion going on at the Indian meeting. Scout Chaney watched them.

"Looks like they got two or three bands together for the hunt and now nobody can figure out who's in charge. No war chief, or more likely four or five war chiefs. But they are damn upset. They wanted to ride us down."

"Figures," Captain Harding said. "They'll decide. They only have six more hours before dusk."

Ten minutes later the Indians broke into a wide front, then half a dozen men rode faster to form a wide "V" so each warrior had a clear shot at the enemy.

They rode forward slowly at first, then as the "V" formed, they came faster and charged straight at the point of the stream where it parted and went down both sides.

"Hold your fire until my command!" Captain Harding shouted. The Comanche war cries shrieked through the afternoon Texas stillness.

One rifle from somewhere in the Indian ranks fired. The savages came closer and closer. When they were fifty yards from the point of the creek, Capt. Harding bellowed: "Fire!"

Forty rifles belched black powder smoke and forty .52 caliber lead slugs snarled toward the Indians. Four of the five Indians riding the point of the "V" either lost their lives or their horses in the first volley.

From then on it was ragged firing as the men pounded out the seven rounds in their Spencer repeaters.

The Indians kept coming, surging into the water and heading straight for the point of the defenses.

Captain Harding lifted his Spencer and sighted in on the jolting form of a Comanche warrior. He fired. The man fell off his horse but the mass of Comanche warriors kept coming. They were only twenty yards away from the point of the island!

16

Sadie Harding sat under a big pecan tree near a stream and pounded the dried buffalo jerky into powder using a hand sized rock to beat against the hard jerky that lay on another rock. When she had the copper bowl filled, she carried it to Cries In The Morning, who was mixing the jerky with buffalo fat and pecans. When it was all mixed and pounded together it became pemmican, the staple of the Indian diet during the winter months.

Sadie emptied her bowl and watched Doris, the only white eye woman in the camp. She and Doris and little white boy called Daniel, had become good friends. They could speak English when the Comanches weren't listening.

Doris pounded jerky, too, and they talked about where they used to live. Doris never talked about the settlement where she was captured. She talked about St. Louis, and Austin.

"We've been pounding this stuff for hours," Doris said. "Don't they ever get enough?"

"This is what we'll eat this winter, when we can't hunt," Sadie said.

"Sweetheart, we won't be here this winter. We have to find a way to get away from the Comanche or we'll both wind up being Indian squaws the rest of our lives. Little Dan thinks he's an Indian already."

They had ridden away from the Croton Creek standoff with the Pony Soldiers. Doris had been taken up the river and tied to a tree until the Pony Soldiers had left. Then she was brought back. For a week they had traveled north and now were on Mulberry Creek, a tributary of the mighty Red River. They were far to the north, almost past the long and massive cap rock that protected the Staked Plains.

They had not seen a white eye since they left Crotin Creek. Not a settler, not a wagon, not a soldier. For the moment they felt safe. But again, White Eagle had posted some of his best warriors as guards. They would not be surprised by the hated Tonkawas again. They were protected, they had found a small herd of buffalo for their last hunt, and the butchering had gone on now for three days.

They had so much buffalo meat to dry that they had to make new racks. Families that had already filled their rawhide boxes with pemmican helped someone else. This was a time of harvest and even the warriors helped the women provide the winter's food supply.

With the mulberries nearly gone from the trees, the band could harvest few of them to flavor their pemmican, but they found every remaining berry. Some late fruiting blackberries were used as well along with the ever present pecans from the wild pecan trees that lined many of the streams.

"Do you think my daddy will ever find us?"

Sadie asked.

Doris stopped pounding the jerky and nodded. "Oh, yes, darling girl, he will, and he'll rescue us and carry us back to the fort and I want to take care of you just like you were my very own little girl, just forever and ever." Tears brimmed her eyes as she thought about her own little girl she had seen the Comanches kill without mercy. "I'll always take care of you, Sadie!"

White Eagle rode in with another horse packed heavily with meat ready to be sliced and hung. He watched Doris a moment as Always Smiling and Talks A Lot unloaded the meat, he walked over to the white woman. She wore a buckskin dress with only a few beads on it. Her dark hair braided on each side.

White Eagle patted her belly and used one of the words he had learned in English.

"Baby?" he asked.

She watched him a moment, then nodded. He grunted and walked away. He had been asking her that question every day now for a month. She would not tell him that she was pregnant before, but now she realized it must be important to him. He must want a son of his own. Doris could not tell him that she could never have any more children. Her last child had messed up the works too much, the doctor told her.

But she would not let White Eagle know. Even that small hold over him might be used to her advantage. She watched the country as they rode north. She knew they must be far to the north in Texas, up in the Panhandle somewhere. Indian Territories were not too far away to the east. But that wouldn't be much help. They would have to get horses and ride east and then south. But how?

No, she would have to wait until the Pony Soldiers came again. But then the Comanches would probably tie her up again, and take Sadie away into the hills so even if the camp were attacked, Sadie would not be there. There had to be a way. There simply had to be! Doris would go crazy if she had to be an Indian squaw the rest of her life.

Four more days of drying the buffalo meat and the rawhide boxes were filled. Now everyone worked at pounding the jerky into pemmican. When the baskets were filled and the boxes overflowing, the whole camp took on a feeling of expectancy. They would soon be going to a winter camp. They were so far north they had no idea where it might be.

That evening White Eagle came to Doris's bed and sat on the edge of it as she fed Daniel. When she finished White Eagle played with the little boy for a while, then settled down to his lesson in English. He was a quick learner. He remembered many more English words than she remembered Comanche.

"Talk English," White Eagle said.

"Good morning, sir," Doris said.

He repeated the words, not sure what they meant. She explained to him with signs and other words. He nodded.

"We must talk about my people," Doris instructed. Day by day she tried to teach him words that he would need if he ever met face to face with white men in some kind of a treaty or bargaining conference. It was happening more and more. Before White Eagle had lived his life out, she was sure he would be pleading with the white men for the good of his people. She could help that much at least.

Deep down she hated him for being part of the savage mob that had tortured and killed her family and friends. But she also realized he had chosen to spare her. She really owed her life to him, and so did small Daniel. It was a strange and discomforting position.

For an hour they talked English. He told her how to say the same thing in Comanche. Sadie sat listening, her quick mind picking up most of the words. She had a natural talent for languages, Doris decided.

White Eagle permitted the instruction for about a half hour more, then he stood.

"I must go now," he said in English, grinned at his own ability and stalked out of the tipi.

He took four of his best ponies, but not his war pony, and tied them in front of another tipi.

A warrior came out of the tipi and stared at the ponies, then at White Eagle.

"These beautiful ponies are for Slender Pecan, your oldest daughter."

The warrior nodded and went back into his tipi. For three hours White Eagle sat in the grass beside the horses. He waited patiently. It was part of the ritual. When a man wanted a girl as a wife, he made an offering of horses to her father. If the father or the girl herself unfastened the horses and walked away with them to her father's herd, the marriage was approved.

After another hour White Eagle was losing hope. Then a slender girl of fifteen came out of the tipi. She wore her finest dress with more than a hundred elk's teeth clicking and making small noises as she walked. She had a round, pretty face, with eyes that never missed a thing. She had already turned down two offers of marriage. This time she walked to White Eagle, smiled at him, then unfastened the horses and led them to her father's string of ponies where the young boys herded them.

That night Slender Pecan came to White Eagle's tipi. There was a bed made ready for her. She was his third wife, and Always Smiling and Talks A Lot were pleased. A war chief should have at least three wives. His white woman and Cries In The Morning did not count, even though he did use the white captive as a wife. Now there would be a boy child in the chief's tipi! It was the fondest wish of the Indian women.

Slender Pecan shivered as she lay under the buffalo robes waiting for her husband. He came to her bed quickly. The fire had died down to a soft glow and no one built it up. Always Smiling and Talks A Lot moved outside into the moonlight to sit beside a small fire and let the new bride have some privacy.

White Eagle slipped in beside her. He had dropped his breechclout and now felt her bare legs against his. His hands found her breasts and her pretty face and he played with her a moment, then pushed her over.

"You must make for us a boy child," he told her sternly. She looked up and nodded. Then he repeated the words over and over again as he thrust deep into her to plant his seed into this new and fertile field. Slender Pecan had two brothers, she knew about males and would be male oriented and would surely bear the chief a male heir.

That day White Eagle had thrown the magic mix of herbs and sacred powders to the four corners of the sky in the ritual appeasement of all the gods he worshipped. He had called on his special god to make him virile and to make his new wife ready to produce a male son.

It would happen. This time it would happen, White Eagle had no doubt.

The next morning the council met. It was time to move to their winter quarters.

"We will winter with our cousins the Mesquite band as usual," Elk Wound said. "But we are not sure where they have made their last hunt."

"They usually work along the Peace River," another warrior said. "We can send a scout to find them."

White Eagle listened to the talk, but always he was thinking that they must stay well away from Captain Two Guns. The man must be half Comanche. He was a worthy opponent. White Eagle knew that he could never go below the Wichita River again. The White Captain must be made to travel many days rides to find the White Eagle band.

But when they made winter camp there would be four, perhaps five bands staying together. No Pony Soldier would dare to challenge two hundred warriors in their winter camp.

He listened to the ideas of the warriors around the council. Soon it was decided to send a rider to find the Mesquite band. Then they would make their plans. They had two or three weeks before the other bands would be moving to winter quarters.

In the tipi Doris sat holding Daniel as he ate pemmican and chewed on buffalo jerky. There had been no fresh meat since the hunt. Everyone was full of red meat for awhile.

Sadie sat near Doris and leaned against her.

"Will we die in the snow this winter?" Sadie asked. She looked up and Doris wanted to hug her.

"No, of course not. The Comanche live through the winter, how else to you suppose they grow so old? We will be snug and safe and warm inside the tipi. You know how the sides come in and we put our beds and buffalo robes on them to shut out the cold. The tipi cover is thick and will keep the fire's warmth inside."

"I would rather be in a house, or at Fort Comfort. That's where my mother was taking us when the bad Indians hurt us."

"Fort Comfort? I'm not sure where that is, but we'll find it someday."

"Then is my daddy really coming to get us?"

Doris blinked back tears. How could she tell her? There was little chance of any large scale cavalry action during the winter. It just had never been done. Which meant she and her two small charges surely would have to stay until the spring or summer before they could get away.

Doris frowned. Within a month or two, White Eagle would know that she wasn't pregant. She had no idea what he would do to her then. She would probably lose her favored status and become a slave. She might even have to sleep outside. No! She would kill herself first!

No! Then what would happen to little Dan and to Sadie? She had to survive, she had to help the children get away from these savages. It was the only course she could take.

17

What now looked like two hundred painted, mounted Comanche warriors stormed the front of the small island in the North Concho River where the forty men of Lightning Company hunkered down firing their Spencer seven-shot rifles as fast as they could.

At twenty yards the toll on the attacking Comanche braves was awesome. Horses went down, others fell over them.

Comanche braves fell from the saddle wounded or dead.

Horses screamed and rushed down both sides of the island without riders.

Suddenly the crush of Comanche at the point broke and the warriors splashed down the shallow stream on both sides, taking more killing shots from the cavalrymen.

"Broke them, by damn!" Captain Harding shouted. Fifty to seventy five of the mounted warriors never came close to the island. When they saw the deadly fire of the guns-that-fire-many-times, they turned and pulled back out of range.

"Let the wounded leave if they can," Captain Harding bellowed.

In front of the island it looked like a slaughter-house.

Twenty braves lay dead. A dozen more crawled slowly back toward the north. Fifteen horses sprawled in the shallow water, half of them dead, the rest with broken legs or serious bullet wounds.

Captain Harding sent two men with pistols out into the water to put the last of the Comanche ponies out of their misery with head shots.

After the mercy blasts the Texas countryside was quiet.

"Load all the magazine tubes you have, men. They'll be back. Let's have a casualty report to Sgt. Casemore by squads."

Captain Harding loaded the three tubes he had that held the six shots of .52 caliber rounds for the Spencer. He hadn't realized he'd used three on the attack.

Now he looked around. He had no memory of the Comanche firing arrows, but there were fifty or sixty arrows he could see stuck in the ground behind the troops, broken on the rocks, and some in tree trunks.

A lot of them must have been shot by riders behind the first wave. They would send them up like a mortar shell hoping the arrows would land on the troops.

Captain Harding picked up an arrow two feet from where he lay and examined it. Straight and smooth, as though it had been turned on a good wood lathe. How did they get them so straight working with shoots of willow?

Sgt. Casemore came up with a casualty report. He had a bandanna wrapped around his left arm. Blood seeped through it and stained his blue shirt sleeve black.

"Sir, we have one man dead, Private Barlow. He took an arrow through the throat and died in seconds. He was on the point. We have eight men with minor wounds, all arrows. All of the eight, including myself, are fit for duty and on line ready for the next charge."

"Damn! Sorry to lose Barlow. He was a good man. Tell the men I'm proud of them, they fought just like we trained to do. Christ, I thought they were going to charge right over us for a few seconds there."

"It was close. I think we put down two or three of their war chiefs. That's going to cause holy hell in the ranks."

Lars Chaney, the free lance scout, pushed up from behind the log he had been using to shoot over. He loaded a tube with rounds.

"Hell, the Comanche ain't done yet. Don't count on no more head on charges, though. Think the hostiles out there discovered the Spencer repeating rifle this afternoon. Probably the first time they seen what it can do." Chaney chuckled. "Give a keg of whiskey to be a mouse in somebody's pocket out there listening to what the Comanches are talking about."

"What do you think they'll do now?" Harding asked.

"Palaver for another half hour. Then they'll wait us out. Once we get out of here and start moving, the odds even up. Fact is they'll have the advantage. Yep. Reckon that's what they'll plan."

In front of them thirty yards, one Comanche lifted up from the water and looked at the island. At last he began crawling through the water to the shore fifteen feet away. On shore he rested a minute, then tried to stand but couldn't. He looked back at the island and the forty guns there, then crawled toward the cluster of Comanche warriors three hundred yards away.

Another Comanche lifted up, and ran flat out for the shore.

Colt Harding brought up his Spencer and knocked him down with his second shot.

"I said the wounded could leave, not some son-of-a-bitch playing dead," Colt shouted to his men. "Now he can leave."

The man hooted and cheered.

Sgt. Casemore looked at the pow-wow. "They might give us one more charge, I don't know, Captain. They sure as hell won't be as confident of overrunning us this time. We took a lot of the fight out of them. I counted twenty-one Redskins out there who ain't moving. That hurts this bunch."

A rifle shot slammed into the island. Missed everyone.

"First squad, one round per man, drive that bunch back a ways. Three hundred yards."

The ten Spencers spoke in a ragged volley. The Comanches reacted at once, galloping out of sight over a small rise.

"Everyone stay down," Sgt. Casemore bellowed. "They are still there and we're still pinned down. We'll be here a while so get comfortable, or work on your barricade. Now's a good time to move some dirt."

Captain Harding looked at his guide. The

Tonkawas had not returned. "Mr. Chaney. How far behind us should our B Company be by now?"

"Sir, at forty miles a day, they should arrive about dusk. A messenger from us to go after B Company would be picked up by the Comanche at once, so we better not try to hurry up B Company any."

"My thoughts. Casemore. Pick out your best man and send him to the back of the island. Keep him in the brush and tell him to watch for B Company. When he spots them he should fire three times in the air."

"Yes sir." Casemore crawled down along the line keeping under cover as much as he could.

"So now we wait," Captain Harding said.

"Think I'll do a little yard work case them Comanches decide to come back," the scout said and moved back to his log. He used a big knife and began digging a shallow trench in back of the log so he could protect himself better.

Captain Harding never saw the man leave for the brush. Good. Probably the Comanche lookouts didn't either.

A half hour later a twenty warrior band of Comanche showed briefly on the rise ahead, then galloped to the west. Ten minutes later another band showed themselves and rode to the east.

"Just letting us know that they're still with us," Captain Harding said.

"About all they can do," Chaney agreed. "Once it gets dark we could pull out. Most of these Comanches don't like to fight at night."

"First we wait and team up with Edwards and Company B. I like the numbers better with fifty more men."

A Comanche rider bolted over the hill and

stormed straight at the island. He stayed on the grass and when he was fifty yards away he wheeled and charged back to the rise and out of sight.

A trooper along the line leaned over the stub of a log to secure it better. He was totally exposed to the Comanche.

Before he could pull back, a Comanche warrior lifted up from behind a dead horse twenty yards away and shot an arrow. Five Spencers blasted the warrior before he could reach for another arrow. He went down in a froth of bloody water and then lay still.

The trooper caught the arrow in his side. He fell back over the log and lay there swearing. The cavalryman next to him checked the arrow. It was in past the barbs and didn't extend through the flesh.

Captain Harding crawled along the troopers to the hit man and looked at the wound.

"Private Fisher, isn't it?"

"Yes, sir. Sorry."

"Don't worry about it. We won't be able to do much about that arrowhead until we get out of here." He drew his knife and notched the shaft on both sides two inches above the flesh. Then before Fisher knew what his captain was doing, Harding broke off the shaft. Fisher groaned and almost passed out.

Captain Harding took a metal flask from his inside pocket and opened the top.

"Take a shot of this now and then, Fisher. Don't give these other troopers any. You'll need all that's there."

"Whiskey?" Fisher asked.

Captain Harding nodded. "All of you, keep

your heads down. B Company should be showing up in an hour or two. Then we'll decide what to do."

For an hour things were quiet. Then a rifle from a hidden position sent six rounds into the small island over a period of five minutes.

The quiet after that was strained. Then the men felt something unusual and at the same time heard it.

"Oh damn! I heard that sound before," Scout Chaney said. "Sir, I suggest we mount up damn fast and get out of here!"

"Why, Chaney?"

"Buffs! That's a buffalo stampede heading this way!"

"To the horses!" Colt bellowed. "Mount up and move out. Buffalo stampede coming!"

The men ran for their horses. Cpl. Swenson had the captain's mount to him in thirty seconds. They mounted and rode to the rear where the other men were mounting.

"There they come!" somebody yelled.

The men looked through the brush and trees upstream and saw a shaggy, brown river as wide as the small valley and every one of the beasts charging downstream. They blanketed the valley and the water, making great geysers of splashes.

"Downstream, to the south," Captain Harding roared again and the troops galloped out of the trees, across the shallow stream and to the banks on both sides, racing forward.

The buffalo thundered on. Slowly the riders began to outdistance the shaggy bison.

Captain Harding fired his pistol twice and waved the men to the left up and across a small hill in an effort to get out of the way of the creatures.

Just as they topped the rise they saw below them fifty Comanche warriors who shouted their war cries and stormed up the hill.

There was no other place for the cavalry company to go.

"Charge!" Captain Harding bellowed. "Pistols, Up!" They were a hundred yards from the hostiles when over the same ridge, a quarter of a mile down appeared a blue ribbon of riders.

The familiar bugle call of "attack" echoed through the small hills, and the Comanches looked up in surprise and anger. The two forces were still fifty yards apart when the Comanche turned with no apparent order and rode away.

Half the troop got in rifle shots at the retreating backs of the Comanche before they vanished over a slight rise.

Three minutes later Company B rode up in a flurry of flapping guideon and shouts of welcome.

Captain Harding rode back up to the brow of the rise and looked down at the small North Concho River. A thundering mass of shaggy brown beasts still poured down the narrow little valley. They smashed flat brush and tore around trees, tipping over many of the smaller ones and trampling them into kindling.

He rode back to his command, checked to be sure he had all of his Lightning men. Private Fisher was grinning, half drunk but able to sit on his horse. He sang a song softly, but nobody minded. Sgt. Casemore reported all men present or accounted for, including the dead trooper, Barlow, tied over his horse which was on a lead line.

Captain Harding shook hands with Lt. Edwards and they both decided it was time to put some distance between themselves and the last hunt of the season for the Comanche.

They rode until it was dark, saw no more sign of Comanches, and only a few straggling knots of buffalo. They camped that night on the highest hillock they could find and kept out double guards.

It was an uneventful night.

Two days later they rode into Fort Comfort. Lt. Riddle met them at the gate.

"Everything's been quiet here. Got the Kenny women off with an escort heading for Austin two days ago. Dispatch rider came in. You have a three pager from Col. Sparkman about your Lightning unit. I get the idea he'll want to come take a look at your men in action before long. He says General Phil Sheridan is interested."

"The hell you say? He'll have to get in line and wait until I'm ready to see him. First I get a bath."

A half hour later, Captain Colt Harding relaxed in his hot bathtub in his quarters. One more mission against the Comanches that did not result in rescuing Sadie. She wasn't at this site, but she had been with White Eagle. He knew it. But the damned Comanche was a good tactician. There was only one way to get Sadie out of that camp before the snow began, and it had to be before the Comanche settled down in a winter camp with as many as three hundred other tipis.

He had to concentrate now on going in with a dozen or so Tonkawas, going in quietly, without an army unit trailing him. Going in and beating White Eagle at his own tricks. That was the only way he would ever see his little girl again. He had three weeks to a month to do it. Now was the time! He had to do it, and he had to do it right now! He'd get started first thing in the morning setting it up.

For the first time in four months, Captain Colt Harding felt he was on the right track. Now he had a chance. He might never return from this probe, this mission, but he would know that he had done every goddamned thing he could to get Sadie back where she belonged, and out of the clutches of Walking White Eagle!

Tomorrow! Just wait until tomorrow!